VAMPIRE UMPIRE

A Novel

by

Ross Macpherson

Dedication

For Laura: a rambling tale of magic and heroism.

"Forget your perfect offering: there is a crack, a crack in everything. That's how the light gets in, and that makes it damn hard to be a vampire."

- Leonard Cohen, *Anthem*, 1992.

Table of Contents

Prologue

A screaming comes across the sky. It has happened before, but there is nothing to compare to it now.

A yellow-green blur, like a cartoon brawl between Kermit the Frog and Homer Simpson, perhaps over the latter attempting to consume the legs of the former, transcribes its arc against the stars and strikes the ground. The ball landing hazes the air with a greyish white powder and simultaneous the crowd's collective breath holds, as if daunted to breathe it in. Actually their respiratory interruption comes from being in one of those rare moments that exist almost outside time where a decision must be made before the flow of reality can resume.

It is championship point in the tennis match, against the previously undefeated player on whose side the ball has landed. Jebediah Moslius casts a sly speculative gaze at the umpire and then pumps his fist as if the point has gone his way, just as the umpire says, "Game, set and match... Molly Durand." The crowd rises as one to their feet, as if all their genitals were chained together and attached to a crane on the stadium roof, but cheer with a full-throated pleasure that suggests that simile is inaccurate.

"That ball was out!' Moslius shouts at the umpire, stabbing towards him with his tennis racquet, "unlike mine with your mother last night."

"The ball was definitely in, I am afraid," the umpire replies, "and if you like I can summon you medical attention, for it has been… many years since my mother passed away."

"I challenge!" On the board where the score now flickers, caught like Schrodinger's Cat between a final state or some potentially endless continuation, the number of challenges allowed to each player when they doubt the umpire's call appears. Molly Durand has all three of hers left; Moslius has zero. Challenges are only lost when the player challenges incorrectly.

"I'm sorry Mr. Moslius but your challenges are all lost, like this tournament for you," the umpire says.

"Now listen to me, you…" Moslius begins when, as quickly as any of her other responses to his actions in the match, Molly Durand speaks up: "I challenge," she says.

The umpire looks at Durand and smiles. "Thank you, Ms. Durand."

"Call me Prince Molladin," she says.

"I never will," says the umpire, "though it is a noble gesture you have made." The challenge system employs immensely high speed cameras, developed for reasons best hand-waved over for filming bukkake, focussed on the mathematically precise lines of the court. The umpire runs the system, with the scoreboard showing the replay for Moslius, Durand, the umpire and the crowd. The film plays.

"I am very sorry, Ms. Durand," the umpire says, "but you now only have two challenges remaining. However, as you have won the match, that seems," he pauses briefly - Moslius has flung his racquet at the umpire's head, faster and more confidently than any shot he has made in the match, and the umpire takes a moment to pluck it from the air as deftly as a Scotchman steals food at a wedding buffet – "that seems somewhat irrelevant."

"Nice shot, Jeb," Durand shouts at the player now chesting through the gathering storm of officials preparing for the award ceremony. "If you'd been as accurate as that earlier, maybe you'd have won!"

The umpire laughs. Durand sits down in her player's chair next to the umpire as the tournament officials unfurl the cerements of the championship's end. "Nice to meet you," she says. Molly had been a shy girl and had overcome her shyness by reading Williams' How To Make Friends But Not Influence People, from which she had learned and made her unvarying habit that on making a new acquaintance it is important to ask them good questions, at which point they will befriend you full on. She says, "What's your name?" and reaches out her hand.

The umpire reaches down to shake. "Vampire Umpire," he says. His ever so sharp and unnaturally long canine teeth glint under the floodlights.

"What the hell!" Durand says, horrorstruck. Vampire Umpire feels his body still as if the grave had finally claimed him forever. "I'm not going to have time to say that all the time. I'll just call you V." He smiles at her and she smiles back and in the sight is all the glory and loveliness of the dawning sun forever denied him.

Chapter One

Tyrone Ennis, great to whatever would be the correct degree grandson of Terrence Ennis (inventor of Tennis) and owner-operator of the International Tennis League, reached across the desk. His white shirt was beautifully cut, immaculately pressed and pristine except for elbows grimed in mud and haloed with grass stains. He noticed Vampire Umpire looking at them. "Oh, sorry," he said. "I just watered my desk this morning."

The desk was a miniature tennis court, accurate enough that it was evidently made of real grass. Bisecting the desk was a small net, strung so that it pointed between the visitor's seat and the desk's owner's chair. "It's very striking," said Vampire Umpire, running one long-fingered hand over the grass, the blades trembling beneath his sharp nails. "But is it not impossible to get anything done on this desk?"

"No, yeah, it's awful for work. All my letters get too soggy to read, and I've lost count of the number of times I've sent someone an invite to a tennis tournament and they've called the police about the maniac sending them what they assume is faeces-encrusted paper through the mail. The Queen even kept me locked in the Tower of London for a week until she was sure it was, in her words, "'the sweet soil of England one has been sent, and not the foul soil of your bowels.'"

"So...?"

"So it turned out it was just earth, and I was released!" Ennis smiled ruefully. "Though ironically, as the toilets in the Tower didn't work, the thank you letter I immediately wrote her was considerably less salubrious."

"I meant more, why not change the desk."

"Oh, but I got released, so it was all fine." Tyrone Ennis waved across the desk, attempting to indicate the matter was fully discussed, though unfortunately in the flamboyance of his gesture his hand became entangled in the net. Somehow he had wound his fingers firmly into the mesh and he and Vampire Umpire spent the next several minutes slowly unpicking them like Christmas lights tangled in the dusty false beard of a false Santa who has collapsed into the family tree and is rapidly ruining Christmas for everyone.

"I mean the desk has some drawbacks," Tyrone conceded.

"Yes?"

"It stirs the envy of all who see it, which is why I have so few friends. Anyway, let us talk of other things." He made the gesture again, but this time Vampire Umpire used his vampire speed to tug the net down before Ennis' fingers could get caught more efficiently than shrimp after a storm by Forrest Gump. "It was such a fortunate coincidence that you happened to be in the crowd when the scheduled umpire missed the match."

Vampire Umpire smiled. "For a… very long time I have loved tennis," he said. "Not playing it, which requires a skill and grace I could never possess, but in enabling the performance, like a catalyst can transform a chemical reaction from failure to fission."

"And with no training, you scored the game flawlessly. Especially when Jeb threw that tantrum. And his racquet. That was a difficult situation, and you handled it exactly as we hoped, including dropping some pretty sweet burns. Listen," Tyrone Ennis leaned briefly forward over the desk before the support post for the net jabbed him in the throat. Choking and coughing he sat back immediately, eventually managing to gasp out, "I found out last night my umpire was murdered. He was found in the canal, entirely drained of blood, yet with only two small puncture wounds in his neck."

Vampire Umpire would have grown pale, had he not already been whiter than a racist ghost. "Golly gosh," he said.

"Exactly what the police said when they found him, I wager. But what I wanted to ask you was: how would you like to replace him and be an umpire on the tennis tour?"

Vampire Umpire was standing before he realised it. Darkness swirled around him like a cloak, and the ceiling of the room disappeared as if under the roiling of black thunder clouds, his long fuliginous cape swirled behind him like devil's wings flapping madly against the imprisoning soil of Dis. "I would really like that so much!" he said.

Tyrone Ennis' mouth was agape and he lay back in the chair as if heartstruck. "My god!" he exclaimed. "I *love* your enthusiasm!"

♦

As he walked out of the office, Vampire Umpire noticed Molly sitting in the waiting area. Outside of her tennis clothes, he realised… Actually on closer inspection, it turned out she was wearing the exact same clothes in which she had competed the day before: a pair of pale blue jeans, blanched white over the thighs, and a terracotta t-shirt with the slogan "no its becky." Her hair was no longer coiled into a crude bun though and cascaded in rich brown curls down over her shoulders. She was eating the last few Pringles from an extra large tube of Texas BBQ flavour. She licked the last one and held it poised delicately between her fingers, like a princess would a fine paintbrush with which she intended to delicately add a few fine details to a portrait of her sovereign. "Sorry, would you like one?"

"I never eat… crisps," Vampire Umpire said.

"Aww, don't be a Grumpy Umpy, Grumpy Umpy," Molly said. "Eat it," she shouted and lunged forward, shoving it straight in his mouth, which seems a remarkably poor choice of phrase.

"DELICIOUS," Vampire Umpire said. "This is so good it automatically makes everyone from Texas seem less gun-crazed and violent and racist than they actually are."

"Too true. And while they have loads of calories," she leaned in and raised one eyebrow, "they'll often give you the runs real bad, so there's almost no consequence to eating them."

"So how did you get into tennis?" Vampire Umpire asked her.

"What's tennis?" she replied.

"You know – the thing you won yesterday?"

"Oh right. Well I only did that by chance. Thanks to one of my ex-boyfriends I discovered I *really* love hitting balls as hard as I can, so I thought why not slightly alter that skill and see if I could win some money."

"Well it turns out you have a real talent for it!"

"Oh yeah, people are always calling me a real ball breaker."

"I guess you do hit them pretty hard," Vampire Umpire said.

"You have no idea," Molly said, and high fived him. "So were they offering you a job, Grumpy Umpy?"

"Actually, yes. I'm joining the tour as an umpire."

"Cool. You probably did really well yesterday. I mean, I don't know any of the rules, but no-one told you off, so whatever happened you got away with it."

"And you?"

"Oh they want me to travel around and play more events for money, they told me. I'm just going to negotiate the contract." Molly paused and looked Vampire Umpire over like he were a dong-heavy dude at a gigolo parlour or a really nice plate of fajitas, with some sour cream, cheese and salsa on the side, so you could have them exactly the way you wanted them. "Listen, I'll be booking travel and hotels super late and it's going to be expensive. Do you maybe want to become my travelling roommate?"

"I'd like that so much!" Vampire Umpire said. "My last roommate was not ideal. He kept feeding flies to spiders and then spiders to mice and then trying to eat the mice."

"So he was overly familiar?" Molly asked, one eyebrow raised like a cantilever bridge.

"Haha, yes. Plus I mean at least if he'd tried feeding the mice to cats first I would have got to play with a kitten."

"I'm not going to lie to you," Molly said. "Unless the next person is *seriously* into bestiality, I like kittens a lot more than the next person. So this… this definitely makes me like you more."

"And he kept trying to take pictures of me in the shower. But I still think the concept of roommates is sound in principle."

"Then excellent. Here's my phone number. I'm gonna get my money from this guy and we'll meet later to sort things out, okay?" Vampire Umpire watched as she barged through the door, shaking his head in admiration at her poise.

◆

Unfortunately, in the Tyrone Ennis Tennis Centre atrium, Vampire Umpire had a less pleasant encounter. Jebediah Moslius was concluding an interview with a film crew when he noticed his new nemesis walking elegantly down the staircase. "And there he is!" the tennis player shouted pointing vigorously. "The idiot who gave me my first ever loss."

"Mr. Moslius, that's not true." Vampire Umpire said. "You were defeated by Molly Durand, who had apparently never played before entering this tournament, so I worry how you will fare when she has more experience."

"You made the wrong calls!"

"I'm afraid I made no wrong calls, unlike the parents who decided to have you, or the doctors who decided to deliver you to anywhere other than the nearest recycling bin."

Moslius stared agape at Vampire Umpire for far too long, while the latter simply waited patiently for a response. It eventually involved a profanity and Moslius storming out of the building. On his way out a young woman grabbed his arm and he angrily shoved her aside. "Sorry for spoiling your interview," he said to the producer for the film crew.

"Haaaaaa. Yeah, nobody is going to want to see footage of a celebrity throwing a tantrum and cursing," the producer said. "You've probably just got me a raise. Of course I'll still be incredible debt, it will just be less emotionally crippling."

Vampire Umpire spoke to the woman Moslius had pushed. "Are you alright, madam?"

"Oh, I'm fine," the woman said. She had dark hair cut short and bound in a ponytail, and a thick Romanian accent that reminded him of the centuries he had spent in Transylvania after the Count had turned him.

"Are you Mr. Moslius'… friend?" he asked.

"I think I'm his girlfriend?" she said. "I was one of the ball people at the match yesterday, and as he left I told him he had played so well and deserved to win, and he told me to come with him because he wanted to see my ball handling skills."

"So he tried to evaluate your ability with a tennis racquet?" he asked.

"I thought so, but when we got to his place it turned out he first wanted me to have sex with him, and after that he fell asleep, so I guess he will test my tennis skills further into our relationship."

"Unfortunate."

Vampire Umpire introduced himself and the woman told him her name was Ioana Dumitrescu. "Can I offer you a lift home?" he asked.

"I guess I should go to Jeb's place," she said. "But thank you, that would be very kind." She held out her hand to shake. Vampire Umpire took it, and recoiled instantly, a cloud of vapour forming around his scalded hand. "Are you okay?" Ioana asked.

"Just an... allergic reaction," he said. "Have you handled a lot of garlic today?"

"No, none," she said. "Oh wait. Actually I kind of do. My father manufactured the world's first and only garlic-scented perfume. It is how we lost all our family money. I wear it to remember him."

"I see," he said. "Well, I will still drive you home, but maybe I'm going to keep my windows open in the car."

"You know it's strange, but all my friends do that," she said. "I guess they have garlic allergies too."

◆

As Vampire Umpire and Ioana were driving out of the centre, a black 1967 Chevy Impala was pulling up to it. Inside were a man and a woman, each more good looking than the last, which might not seem to make sense, but basically if you looked at one you'd go "Dang they're good looking," and then you'd look at the other and say "But they're even *better* looking," and then you'd look back at the first and opine, "Except this one is far lovelier," and this would continue at length until someone interrupted you or you'd hit the word count you wanted for your chapter. Thankfully someone just tapped me on the shoulder and I got out of that sentence with my dignity and the rules of grammar intact.

The pulchritudinous siblings were Jean and Ham Remington. Ham was the younger of the two, and the more garrulous. But when his older sister chose to speak, he obeyed quickly. In some ways she was his opposite: terse, generally visibly angry and she kept her blonde hair cut short while her brother's brown hair rambled as long and freely as his sentences (and sometimes mine). But they agreed fervently on their commitment to their business.

"You get the kit, Jean," Ham said. "We're going to need evidence to convince this Ennis guy."

"Why d'we need to convince him? Let's just do the job and move on."

"Because we're out of money and he might pay us? You can't fuel this thing on monster blood."

"Fine," Jean said, sneering. "I'll get the box of elongated teeth and you can go in there and we can tell him his umpire wasn't just murdered, but that vampires are real and one of them killed him, and then he's going to cut us a huge cheque to save them all. That is definitely what is going to happen."

Chapter Two

Tyrone Ennis stepped up to the microphones that were clustered around the press podium like robot penises at some kind of robot orgy where poor planning had lead there to be only one female robot and none of the male robots were at all heteroflexible. "I have an announcement," he began. "These brave investigators just showed me evidence that vampires are real and told me one of them killed my recently murdered umpire, so I have cut them a huge cheque to save us all." Behind him, Jean and Ham stood, trying to look both cool, competent, dangerous and sexy, which is hard to pull off but they were doing so as thoroughly as the most enthusiastic onanist.

"Told you," Ham whispered.

"Yeah, yeah," Jean said and growled.

"These heroes will be flying out to join the tennis tour at its first stop, in Scotland this week, and they have my full authority to investigate this matter to the best of their handsome and sexy abilities," Tyrone continued. "Now, I am sure you all have questions but I am equally sure I can anticipate those questions: why does my hair look so good, and can your hair look equally good? And the answers are argan oil leave in conditioner and yes, but be sure not to use too much or your hair will be greasier than the sauces at a bad Italian restaurant. And now, since you will have no other questions, good day to you."

He headed back inside the entirely figurative bowels of the Tyrone Ennis Tennis Centre. From off camera, reporters could be heard in a cacophony of colliding voices, saying, "Vampires are real?", "Is this a joke?", "He believes in vampires?", "Argan oil, eh? His hair did look fantastic." and "Who are these clowns, does anyone know?" The last comment apparently irked Jean, who began striding towards whomever had spoken right as Molly turned off the television on which she and Vampire Umpire had watched the broadcast.

"Does this worry you at all, Vumpire?" she asked.

"What?" Vampire Umpire had rarely in his centuries of life felt lost for words, or been failed by his quick mind. But now terror had struck him like a snake strikes someone who has consistently and publicly besmirched snakes for many years.

"Well yeah, like your name is Vampire Umpire. You wear a vampire cape. You have fangs. You sometimes turn into a mist in the bathroom."

"That was just steam. I'd gone out to get shaving foam."

"Oh, right. But still… You never go out during the day. Wolves are constantly bringing you tribute. All these things made me suspicious." Molly said, her eyes narrowing. "But I knew for sure last night, when we went to dinner and I ordered garlic bread and *you didn't have any garlic bread.*"

"Gosh darn it," Vampire Umpire said, and shook his head sadly.

"Yeah," said Molly, "garlic bread is delicious."

"Will you give me time to run?" he asked.

"Why would you run? I don't care if you're a vampire. Actually it's good for me."

"Because I'll never steal the garlic bread?"

"Bingo, Vumpire," she said.

"And you aren't worried that I killed that umpire?"

"Of course not. You may be a vampire but you're clearly a nice dude."

"Thank you, Molly. If I can ever do anything for you, you only need ask."

"You know what I want," Molly said. She stared at him meaningfully and tapped her hips with her hands.

Vampire Umpire sighed. "Fine," he said. "I'll call you Prince Molladin. But only for the rest of the day."

"Excellent," she said. "Now let's go see some of the sights of Aberdeen!"

◆

They were downing their third old-fashioneds at a subterranean cocktail bar styled like a speakeasy when Vampire Umpire said, "Don't you have a match tomorrow morning?"

"Oh yeah!" Molly said. "I completely forgot about that, but I'm sure it will be fine. It's not for another…" she checked the time on her phone, "8 hours, so we still have at least 7 hours to party."

"You really do love to party."

"Oh sure, do you know it's the only time I've been in legal trouble?"

"No? What happened? You get too rowdy and burn down a town, or unleash a plague of rats in one of your drunken black outs?"

"Umm, no," said Molly. "Jeez. I was just gonna say like I was in court once and a judge asked who was 'the guilty party,' and I said I was guilty… of being a party animal." She shrugged. "But before I got out the second clause a bailiff was taken away and I ended up nearly being charged with obstruction of justice. Anyway, more cocktails!"

Around 2 am the bar closed and they walked out onto the street. Vampire Umpire had paid the bartender to make them one more cocktail each, and they were carrying the fine crystal glasses along the cobblestone street uphill, towards a war memorial that consisted of an over-sized lion. Black clouds stretched wispy fingers across the pale full moon, and far in the distance they could hear drunks howling.

"Hey hey," Molly said. "You might be a pretty classy dude, but are you as classy as me?" She raised one eyebrow high, executed a small and slightly too oscillatory to convince bow, and said, "Good day sir," while waving her bent elbows in the air and shaking her hands.

Vampire Umpire laughed so hard he ended up doubled over like a pig in David Cameron's basement, and he was slapping his thighs and laughing when he heard Molly begin to topple. He managed just to grab her before she hit the ground and lifted her onto his shoulders.

"Nooooo!" she yelled. "I want to ride the lion, not you!"

"Mannnn," said Vampire Umpire. "This is bringing me a lot of flashbacks to when I took my ex to Disneyland."

"Onwards, Drunkpire Vamgyre!" she yelled, and bopped him on the head a couple times, just to show him how it would go if he didn't move fast enough.

Unfortunately she had forgotten his vampire speed, and when they arrived at the lion under a second later, she felt like her drinks were going to ride it before her.

"Awww man, I want to vomit, but it was such good whiskey it would be a waste."

"We can buy more whiskey! Oooooh, or I could turn into steam and steal some from the bar!"

"But then wouldn't the body steam and the whiskey steam mix as you stole it?"

"Awww man! Great great call! I'd probably get drunk and sex up a cloud!"

"Don't do that, buddy. You can do, here, help me up," she was half straddling the lion and pushed down hard with her hand on Vampire Umpire's head, "thanks. You can do a lot better."

"Really?" Vampire Umpire looked up at her hopefully.

She looked down, sad and serious, and placed her hand firmly on his shoulder. "Vampure Unfire," she said. "I am MUFASA, Biggest of All The Lions for I have slaughtered ALLLL the other lions! With my bared teeth!" She started gnashing at the air and making small roaring sounds, which more resembled an angered chainsaw than a noble beast who would be a shining example to any human leader. Vampire Umpire sat at the foot of the lion and stared off across the city. There was a park nearby filled with tall trees around which golden lights had been wrapped, like stars dragged low from the heavens ensnared by a net. A nearby building was under-lit by lights that cycled slowly back and forth between neon green and Prince purple like waves crashing over it and rolling back.

Again, the drunks howled in the distance, though closer now. Vampire Umpire watched the moon ripple in one of the oil-slick puddles on the road, fat and white as a Scottish child, but unlike a Scottish child entirely full. He listened again. His icy blood would have chilled in his veins if it were not already, y'know, icy. "Molly," he said. "I think we need to leave here, fast."

"But why?" she said, angry. "Are you saying that so you get a go at being Mufasa? Because I will always be Mufasa." She narrowed her eyes. "Not you."

"I am afraid we might have picked a poor night to party," he said, holding up one hand to defray Molly's immediate interjection that it was never a poor time to party. "More than vampires walk the night in secret. And tonight, the night of the full moon, belongs to the hunt of the werewolves."

"Werewolves?" Vampire Umpire nodded. "Aww man," Molly said. "I really don't like it when a guy is too hairy. Let's get out of here."

"I can't use my vampire speed," Vampire Umpire said.

"Why not? You wearing shoes without proper sole support?"

"Well yeah, but also an object moving as fast as I can disturbs the air. It would carry our scent all over the city, and they'd track us down like Donald Trump tracks down a lady crotch, and grab us just as viciously." Molly's face blanched with horror. "And sorry to say, vampires and werewolves don't get on."

"No? Why not?"

"Well, you know how some people are cat people and some people prefer dogs?"

"Yeah," Molly said.

"Well it's basically that. Vampires love cats, werewolves dogs, and we just never see eye to eye. It kills thousands of each of our kind every century."

They jogged as quietly as they could through the sleeping city, but at every turn that lead back to their hotel the pack sounded closer. "Down here," Molly said, and turned down an alley that ran adjacent to the main street. There was silence as they neared the end, then, just as they prepared to turn back onto the main street about half a kilometre from the hotel, a scream came from straight ahead. They turned, but the pack was behind them as well.

"Here," Molly said, and dragged Vampire Umpire into the space between a wall and a large dumpster, in local parlance known as the Scotchman's spare bedroom. From both sides, through the cloak of night they watched, Molly's breath held, as the beasts slowly approached. Red eyes gleamed in the dark like rubies. Red teeth too, red like fresh blood. One snout scented the air and bent towards them, and Molly felt her nails clench in her friend's shoulder.

And then a car was barrelling towards them. Ham Remington opened the rear door and yelled "Get in," and they were driving away.

"Thank you," Vampire Umpire said. Molly eyed him, then the investigators and seeing he was calm, said "Yeah, thanks."

"Oh," said Ham. "You guys are on the tour, right?"

Jean sighed loudly. "Do the homework, Ham. That's Vampire Umpire and Molly Durand. Read a file from time to time."

"Doing my homework is why I'm the one with a high school diploma," Ham replied.

"You know I left school to look after you when Dad was working!"

"Then what was the nanny for?"

"Fine. Fine, Ham. But if you're so smart, how come I'm the one with the driver's licence?"

"Because of my epilepsy!"

Distracted by the argument, neither of them noticed the monster looming up in front of the car. Molly and Vampire Umpire had, but their frequent interjections and shoulder tapping had been ignored. The car plowed through the werebeast like a vegan through a secret ice cream cone. It was reduced to a few small shreds of flesh, a smear of blood and some scattered shards of bone. One of the last of these managed to puncture the radiator in the engine. "God dammit, Ham," Jean said. "This is all your fault."

Ham was expostulating an aggrieved "What?" right as Vampire Umpire said, "Okay, we need to get to the hotel."

"There's a shelter across the city. We've been driving people there all night," Ham said.

"Yeah," said Molly, "but I get a breakfast if we get to the hotel. Plus my own bathroom."

"Strong argument," Jean said. The beasts' cries came from all around them now, a continuous unbreakable horde closing in on them.

"Okay," said Vampire Umpire. "Let's go as fast as we can, and stick together. If we're even a bit lucky we should be fine."

They got caught about a minute later. On the roofs around them appeared a throng of the creatures, and a small group began to walk down the street towards them. The red eyes and teeth loomed out again first, then the clop of their hooves on the ground and finally, the soft, white outline of their fuzzy wool, glowing gold in the sodium streetlights.

"What the fuck?" Vampire Umpire said.

"Were-sheep?" Molly said.

"Did you not know?" Jean asked.

"Oh for goodness sake!" Vampire Umpire said and strode into the sheep, swinging his arms hard left and right. Molly joined him, and together they had quickly dispatched the entire group of, well, I guess for simplicity's sake, let's say monsters. Up close, the redness in their teeth was revealed to be a mix of red cabbage and carrot, pillaged ruthlessly but harmlessly from local gardens and farms. In fact few of the sheep were able to overcome their bucolic nature enough to make any attempt to attack either Molly or Vampire Umpire, and the one or two who did found that their soft paws and herbivorous teeth did not make for the most efficacious weaponry.

"Whoa," said Jean and Ham together.

"Why didn't we try that, Jean?"

"Well, I mean… They got lucky. They're not overburdened with training on how to be a good paranormal investigator, so they can act without being aware of all the mistakes they might have made."

"You're right, Jean. That was all beginner's luck. I love you." The siblings hugged, taking comfort in their familial bond and their shared competence and superiority to the amateurs now standing watching the defeated horde of were-sheep either bowing in submission or slinking off.

"Okay, warm bath at the hotel?" Vampire Umpire said.

"Sounds good to me!" said Molly.

◆

In the hotel café the next morning, Ham handed Molly a coffee. "It all began over one hundred years ago," he began, at which point her phone went off.

She checked it, then said, "Oh sorry, I forgot I'm meant to be playing tennis right now. Can I meet you back here in like an hour?"

♦

In the hotel café that afternoon, Ham handed Molly a coffee. "It all began over one hundred years ago," he began then waited.

"Please, continue," she said, staring into his gorgeous dark eyes and looking at his perfect face. "You tell the story so handsomely."

"A local Aberdeen man was travelling around Borneo looking for a lost treasure."

"I think it's called Myanmar now, you stunningly lovely slight racist," Molly whispered.

"He ended up losing his money, and his family thought his life. But he returned to the family years late, with terrible scars all over his body."

"A weresheep?"

"A werewolf. But, unfortunately, he had what they call the Lust of Aberdeen. In a few weeks he had lain with a sheep, and spread it his curse. And ever since, Aberdeen has laboured under a terrible invasion every full moon. Well, at least until you and your friend intervened last night, I guess." He ran one muscular hand through his charcoal brown hair, sweeping a soft frond back from over his eye to tuck it behind his ear. He smiled, and two perfect dimples formed in his immaculately high-boned cheeks. Molly wondered if she could fit her tongue in them.

"You make me lust," Molly said. "Uhhhh, after more knowledge of the esoteric." Good save, she thought to herself, and made a note to high five herself later.

"Thanks!" Ham said. He sipped from his coffee cup and it was too hot. A little spilled, decorously, onto the saucer, and he stuck out his tongue and blew on it. Molly laughed and leaned in, and they talked the rest of the day.

Chapter Three

The Grand Imperial Hotel stands atop a riverside cliff in the country just outside of Vienna. The best rooms have windows looking out over the long fall down to the river Danube below, the building being high enough that the rapid passage of the water, which has over centuries etched a deep furrow into the ground, becomes a gentle burble to the ears of the sleeping. The thick forest surrounding the hotel thins tolerably in the autumn, like Barack Obama's hair in the twilight of his presidency, but in the spring and summer grows thick and overgrown and dark, which might be why the rooms are somewhat affordable for an umpire and a novice, if highly naturally skilled, tennis player.

The concierge handed them the room key. "Can I have someone take your bags?"

"No offence, bub," Molly said, "but why would I want my bags stolen?"

"No, Molly, he means…"

"Is it like an insurance scam?" she asked. "You sell the stuff, give me half the profits and I claim whatever the insurance will pay? But what about my no-claims bonus, huh?" She grabbed the concierge's lapels. "What about that?"

"He means to the room? So we don't have to?"

"Ohhhhhh," she said.

"Yeah."

"So you're not going to steal them at all?" she asked the concierge. "Because there's something I don't like about you, chum." She loomed over the concierge, who was a hunched gentleman in his late seventies, with two long moustaches that drooped down white like an aged sine wave across his mouth. His large bulbous glasses just barely made visible the pale blue eyes almost lost in the wrinkled folds of his face. Molly tapped her finger hard on the desk twice. "Yeah, I'm gonna keep my eye on you."

"Why don't I carry our bags?" Vampire Umpire said.

The concierge led them to the rococo lift and shifting his entire body weight into the task, just barely managed to close over the metal grill. He worked the old lever over to the Up position and with a creak the cage rose slowly skyward. He timed the stop perfectly, and the lift bobbed once and settled at the 7th floor.

"I'll get it," Molly said when he went to open the lift. "Don't want to be stuck in here 'til I'm as old as you, guy." She hurled open the door with a rattle that sent metal flakes flying and then stepped into the hall. The walls were draped lusciously in thick red wallpaper, with gold filigree flecking the cornicing, which Vampire Umpire noted was small carvings of cherubim flanking various religious symbols. He would have to be careful not to touch the ceilings, but realistically that was unlikely to be a problem, as his impeccable manners meant he very rarely wandered around fingering the basic furnishings of places. The carpet was a thick wool, burgundy as fresh blood.

The concierge let them into their room and tried to show them the facilities. "Holy hell, what are these 'light switches' of which you speak?" Molly said. "And running water that you operate with something called 'taps'? PLEASE, show me how both those work."

"Thank you," Vampire Umpire said. "I think we'll be fine from here."

"What are you doing tonight?" Molly asked as they unpacked once the concierge had departed.

"The Remingtons want to interview me."

"Get some shirtless pictures of Ham," Molly said quickly.

"What did you say?"

"I said, aren't you nervous?"

"Oh, well, I will see what happens. I'm more worried about the match tomorrow."

"Why? You're not the one playing."

"Yeah, but it's during the day. That was okay in Scotland where they don't have the sun, but here it could be a problem." Vampire Umpire placed his comb on the dressing table in front of his bed and then looked through the wardrobe. He'd hung up his entire wardrobe, which to Molly's eyes consisted of nine identical tuxedos, white shirts, and beautifully cut suit trousers. He however, seemed to perceive some difference, and he selected one outfit very carefully before replacing it and taking another instead. Modestly he went into the bathroom to change, and from there his voice drifted sonorous and ensorcelling, "And your plans for the night?"

Molly felt the hypnotic powers of his voice at work. She felt an overpowering urge to bare her neck and let Vampire Umpire feast on her blood, and she realised that was all she wanted to do tonight. "You're doing it again," she said.

"Oh, sorry." His head appeared around the bathroom door, the collar of his shirt gaping wide. "It's just a natural instinct. I release you from my enchantment." He waved one hand, curling the fingers oddly, and Molly's desire to give him her blood was replaced with a desire to watch Seinfeld and eat a lot of popcorn.

"Oh you know," she said. "I'll probably read, work on my tennis knowledge. I think I finally figured out scoring." She idly noticed Vampire Umpire's comb on the windowsill and picked it up and ran it through her hair a few times. "Hey, you don't know the wifi password do you? Definitely not for Netflix, just for email. I gets a lot of email and I need to reply because of politeness. I wouldn't want people sitting around and waiting in case I want them to enlarge my penis."

Vampire Umpire walked out of the bathroom. His hair was perfectly coiffured into a side parting as severe as a governess' judgement, and his eyes shone like emeralds against the flawless white marble of his face. His outfit was as impeccable as if he were the plastic groom atop a wedding cake. "It's 'wifi password'," he said.

"Did you vampire mind read that hideous old bastard?" Molly asked.

"In a way, I did. It's written on this card," he said and passed her the white slip from the desk. As he walked out the door he said, "Oh, and I ordered you some popcorn as we were checking in."

◆

Jean and Ham met him in a bar near the hotel. The walls were composed of ancient mahogany that was dark as badly tempered plain chocolate and just as riddled with cracks. The ceilings were high and and thickly dusted with both shadows and actual dust, and light came only from sparse suspended light bulbs enwrapped in black velvet shades. The room was lined with booths comprising slightly sticky tables and leather seats gone satiny from overuse.

"Hey," Ham said. "We ordered you two drinks because we weren't sure what you'd want." He gestured with his hand at a tall glass filled with a frothy golden fluid. "Here we have a beer, and here" he gestured at a glass filled with a thick red material, "we have a tomato juice."

Vampire Umpire stared at them for a moment. Jean was visibly tense, and clutching something under the table that he assumed was a stake and not in fact a crudely carved dildo with which she was boldly challenging social convention by carrying it around openly as her boyfriend. "I'll take the delicious beer, please," he said. Jean relaxed instantly, and Ham smiled his big open smile.

"Yeah, we thought as much, but you understand we had to test you to make sure you weren't the vampire, Vampire Umpire." Ham said.

"You're probably the person we suspected least," Jean said. "But vampire hunters aren't like American elections – we can't afford mistakes."

"So you're sure I'm not the vampire now?"

"Oh for defs," Ham said. "No vampire could resist the possibility that that tomato juice might be delectable human blood, served by some kind of appalling kitchen or bar mistake."

"Thank you," Vampire Umpire said. "It is nice that you trust me."

"We know you're not the vampire, Vampire Umpire," Jean said, "but we want you to help us catch them."

"Of course I will help find whoever killed my predecessor," he said. "You need merely tell me what you wish me to do."

"Well," said Ham, "have you any idea who the vampire is?"

"None, I'm afraid." Vampire Umpire thought, after all, does anyone ever really know themselves?

Jean slammed a fist on the table. "Damn! Then we're totally out of ideas. We're just going to have to watch to see if the vampire strikes again."

"We will find who killed the umpire," Vampire Umpire said. "I swear it by my centuries of life. Also, Ham, I think my friend Molly likes you."

◆

Vampire Umpire took a stroll around the town of Talln. His vampire sense of smell was stronger than that of most humans, and the many tubs of flowers and shrubs produced a combined scent that irritated his nostrils. It was overly floral, and reminded him of the abundance of blossoms that filled the hall and flanked the coffin at large funerals. By the fountain at least the flow of water washed the atmosphere a little cleaner, and he sat on the edge for a while, just listening to the night settle over the world. Before long he had lost himself in the long halls of his memory.

His peace was interrupted by the sound of squabbling, in English and near by.

"You never do what I want to do," a man was shouting.

"I'm sorry Jeb, but I would prefer not to have sex in the fountain."

"But it would save me a lot of time getting you wet," Jebediah Moslius shouted.

Ioana said, "Oh, I hadn't thought of that. And I guess you do need to save energy for tennis tomorrow."

"You're right, baby. And that means you're going to have to do all the work, too, remember."

"Okay!" she said.

At that moment, Vampire Umpire felt it would be better to leave. He stood and both Ioana and Moslius gasped.

"Vampire Umpire!" the woman said. "It's good to see you again." She ran over to him and hugged him hard. Her arms around him felt warm and welcoming, and he felt simultaneously both more and less aware of his body. A tightness (of excitement?) formed in the ball of his stomach. It was only when he felt the skin of his neck, where her hands rested begin to scald and slough off that he realised her garlic perfume was killing him.

Shakily he stepped back, swaying and weak. "The pleasure as always is mine, Ioana," he said hoarsely.

Unfortunately, Moslius chose this moment to shove him, saying "Stay away from my side piece, you dick." Vampire Umpire stumbled backwards, tripped over the balustrade of the fountain and plunged into the water. Instantly he felt better, the water having washed off the lingering traces of garlic, but Moslius and Ioana were already moving away, the woman clearly reluctant judging by the way he dragged her wrist along in his thick hands.

"What is a side piece?" she was asking.

"Well, like the girl you keep beside you, baby. You know how it is."

◆

Molly was halfway through the popcorn before she realised. It was salt and sweet, like a diabetic's sweat, and delicious. She was just finishing the fourth and best season of Seinfeld. Beside her, covered in a scurf of popcorn kernels and powdery flavourings, was a book called the Rules of Tennis that, had it been human, would have had perfect sensation all over its body, because it had a spine that had clearly never been cracked.

She paused the episode to go to the bathroom, but when she came back the video was playing again. Ah well. She scrubbed the player back a bit, but it immediately jumped back to the original position. She tried again, and no effect, except that the trackpad on her MacBook suddenly grew so hot she couldn't touch it. She decided to leave it, and she climbed back up on the bed, propping her back against the pillows. She placed the laptop across her thighs and rested the bowl on her stomach.

She reached in, but the popcorn was done. Had she finished it? Why hadn't Vampire Umpire ordered her more? What a douchebag, she thought, her eyes shrunk narrow in anger. She tossed the bowl onto the bedside table and pulled the laptop closer to her. Coincidentally she hit an act break in the episode and the screen went dark. A woman appeared in reflection, her long dark hair braided, her hands spectral and pale and reaching out for the screen.

Molly jumped and looked behind her, but of course there was only the wall. She shivered, but realised the reflection must have been of her. She shook her body deliberately, trying to clear her head, and went back to watching the episode.

The hotel wifi sucked, she decided. There was a weird audio feedback effect occurring. Whenever the studio audience laughed there would be occasionally a second where a single laugh continued, just a little longer than it should. A joke would be said on screen, the audience would laugh and this one high, girlish laugh would continue on for a beat or two after. One time she paused the episode and she would swear the laugh rolled out for just a second after she hit pause.

More than half the night was gone, and the hotel was silent but for her. She wanted to sleep, but for some reason didn't want to stop the episode, or even to turn out the light. With Vampire Umpire still away, she rationalised, it would be rude to let him come back to a dark room. Of course as a vampire, his night vision was sharper than hers during day, but if the Williams' book of friendship had taught her anything it was that total and absolute politeness was one of the twenty eight essential keys to making a friend.

The room lights flickered, and Molly felt her hands clench on the laptop. The lights flickered again and this time the room stayed dark. She could hear herself breathing, hoarse and heavy, and she thought she felt a smooth hand brush down the hair on the side of her face. She leapt out of bed and cracked her knee against the dressing table and fell. Panicked, she crawled towards the door. It flew open as she neared it.

Vampire Umpire stood back lit by the lights in the hall. She grabbed him in a hug.

"Are you okay?" he asked.

"Fine," she said. "I just got spooked. My god – why are you so wet?"

"Normally I'm the one asking that question," he said, smarmily raising one eyebrow, before explaining. And to be clear, explaining why he was wet, not the hilarious joke he had made, which needed no explanation.

"That's tough, Dampy Vampy," Molly said.

"Anyway, it's late, and we both have matches tomorrow," he said. "We should sleep."

Vampire Umpire tucked Molly into bed. "Thanks Dampy Vampy," she said sleepily.

"Good night, Molly. Would you like the children of the night to sing you to sleep?"

"That would be nice," she said. Vampire Umpire's eyes turned inward, and he walked to the window and opened it. On the other side of the river a wolf pack had gathered, and he motioned his hands in small, sculptural gestures like a conductor drawing sound out of an orchestra.

The wolves howled a complex melody in concert. Molly supposed that if she were charitable it would sound like Fur Elise, but she very rarely felt charitable and what it actually sounded like was an angry wolf pack crudely howling. "That's... probably enough," she said.

Vampire Umpire dismissed the wolves, and closed the window. As Molly's eyes fluttered shut, she saw him roll deftly under the bed. Every night he placed a long heavy quilt over the duvet and the ends hung down and kept him shaded from the sun. That she would have to remember to place the Do Not Disturb sign when she woke was her last thought before she drifted into a sleep heavy with troubled dreams.

Chapter Four

Molly was being smothered. Plaster collapsed in on her, filling her mouth, her lungs, closing out the world slowly but inevitably until she was lost in the dark. She woke, to find she was pressing her pillow hard into her mouth, like someone masturbating in their parents' house and doing it pretty well.

She breathed slowly and heavily until she felt her heart calm to a normal rate, also like a familial home masturbator, then said, "Are you awake?"

"Are the curtains closed?"

She checked. "Yes." Vampire Umpire rolled out from under the bed.

"Are you okay?"

"Just a nightmare," she said. "So what are you going to do about your match today?"

Vampire Umpire smiled slightly. "Oh, well the thing about living for centuries is that you gain quite the understanding of human psychology," he said.

"So?"

"So, like a master of macchiavellian manipulation, I will use my skills to delay the match until night falls. Observe." Vampire Umpire took his phone off charge and looked up the number of the first player in his contacts. The call went through and he said, "Good morning, Bruce Sprungfeld?"

"Yeah," said the voice on the other line.

"I'm just calling to confirm that the match will start in two hours on court one."

"Thank you, I'll be ready. I'm not hitting my shots great right now but I'm moving really well, so I guess you could say I feel born to run," Bruce said.

"That's excellent news," Vampire Umpire replied. "I have no idea why Matt Berninger said you were a big dork."

"He called me a dork?" Bruce asked, furious. "Tell him I'm not playing until he apologises."

"I will call him up and see what he says." Vampire Umpire disconnected and dialled the number for the other player. "Good morning Matt," he said. "I hope you're ready to play: the match starts in two hours on court one."

"I'm just cleaning my teeth," Matt said, "so that they will sparkle bright as trophies on the court."

"Well be careful with the toothpaste tube," Vampire Umpire said. "You wouldn't want to swallow the cap or anything."

"Huh, *don't* swallow the cap," said Matt Berninger. "If I ever become an alternative rock musician noted for his profound and poetic lyrics, I will probably use that on my fifth or sixth album, depending on how you count EPs."

"I count the EPs with original material but not the ones that are just live versions," said Vampire Umpire. "Also, delicate issue but have you showered? Because Bruce Sprungfeld was saying you smell so bad he sometimes can't breathe and worries he will pass out while playing."

"He said that?" Matt asked, at least as furious as Bruce had been. "Tell him I'm not playing until he apologises."

"You got it," Vampire Umpire said. "I have a feeling he probably won't back down until around five or six o'clock tonight though."

"The tremendous existential fear that comes with the dark does usually make people apologetic," Matt said. "Okay, we'll give it until then."

"Goodbye to you," Vampire Umpire said.

"And a goodbye to you, too. It was nice speaking to you," said Matt. Both of them disconnected at the same time, meaning neither had hung up on the other. Ordinarily this kind of exchange might get elided as unimportant to the story, but arguably it helps encourage people to be more mannerly by including this kind of detail in fiction.

"And there you go," said Vampire Umpire. "Problem solved."

"I worry," said Molly, "that if you ever used your powers of manipulation for evil, the world would be a terrible place indeed."

"Eh, it's not really my steez," said Vampire Umpire.

♦

Molly, not being as photophobic as her vampire friend, had no reason to postpone her match for the day. However, it did get delayed briefly by virtue of their being a Belgian waffle place en route to the tennis club. The first five Belgian waffles she had soaked in Nutella. The waffles, cooked fresh, turned the Nutella into a molten river that bathed every taste bud in her mouth in pure pleasure. Being aware she was about to undertake a sporting endeavour, though, she had the next five with honey, believing it would give her the natural energy and pep of an industrious bee.

She was only a half hour late when she arrived at the tennis club, but then there was a moderately large kerfuffle when she asked to borrow one of the club's racquets, never having bought one of her own. The club took this request as rather unorthodox, but eventually one of the members was called and agreed to loan her a racquet for the match.

She stepped onto the court in a T-shirt covered in pictures of fish and emblazoned with the slogan "I'm quite the catch" and a pair of cut off jean shorts that she had stolen from an Arrested Development fan she used to date. She swung the borrowed racquet back and forth in the air like a sword, then walked up to where they usually wanted her to stand when the other player began playing. "Let's bang this out," she shouted over to her opponent, who had been stretching and now was transcribing the elegant butterfly motions of various tennis strokes in the air.

"Can we not warm up first?" he asked.

"Are you kidding?" she said. "It's already so hot, my balls are floating in sweat."

"Tennis is meant to be a sport of elegance and grace!" her opponent protested.

"What's yer point?" she shouted back. "I can't talk about my balls, just cos you're feeling all snooty and got yours in a twist?"

"I am going to take pleasure in thoroughly beating you."

"Hey, we can fight after we've played tennis, pal. But I hope you like the flavour of hand, because I'm a bit tasty with my fists."

"I meant *at* tennis," the man said.

"Sure you did. You're just backing down because I scared you with my sass," Molly jeered.

"Let's play!" the guy screamed furiously across the court, like a milkmaid milking a cow that had no milk.

"I'm ready!" Molly screamed back, "Only first, I need to lie down and have one of those lines-guys rub my belly for the next twenty to thirty minutes, because damn those waffles were delicious but they were surprisingly filling too."

The umpire granted her slightly unusual request, and after about thirty-five minutes of Molly lying, sprawled on the grass of the court and groaning like an old sailing ship with splitting beams about to founder at sea, while an audience of five thousand watched with polite interest, the match could begin. After about another thirty-five minutes the match had ended.

"Game, set and match, Ms. Durand," the umpire intoned into his microphone.

"I won?" Molly asked. "Then take that, other player." In fact, the other player had already packed away his racquets and gear and was halfway off the court. Molly picked up a ball and was about to hit it hard into his back when she wondered if that would be entirely sporting. She decided that it was, and would be a good demonstration of skill. He screamed in pain and briefly fell to his knees from the force of the blow, and, while she could no longer remember why she had disliked him, she felt he had probably thoroughly learned his lesson.

The tennis tour manager was walking up to her with a microphone and she decided to get ahead of the story. "I didn't mean to hit him," she said. "The racquet just slipped in my hand."

"What? Oh, no-one cares about that, do we?" The manager raised her arms and gestured around the court and the crowd rolled cascades of applause down on them. Blimey, Molly thought, they must have hated that guy as much as I did for some reason.

"Thanks a lot," she said into the microphone. "I think we all agree I did the right thing."

"Indeed. Not many players win one golden set, let alone three."

"A… golden set?"

"Yeah, exactly."

"Listen I don't know what you think this is but it's sweat on my thighs, not my own urine. I've been toilet trained since my second year of school," Molly said. They didn't need to know she meant high school.

"No, Ms. Durand…"

"And if this is some kinky Austrian fetish thing, I don't play that way. I mean sure, sometimes on a hike, if I feel the need, the need for pee, and the toilet is far away, I'll go in a bush, and yeah, accidents happen. But I'm not into urine stuff during sexy times, I swear."

"Ms. Durand, a golden set is when you win a tennis set without your opponent winning a point. It has nothing to do with urine-based sex acts."

"Ohhhhhhhhh," said Molly. "Ummm, would you believe I knew that and was just joking hilariously?" The manager shook her head sorrowfully. "Then, sorry."

"It is quite the achievement, one few players ever manage in their entire career. We all know you're the newest player on the tour, and with performances like this we're thrilled to see what you will accomplish" the manager said. "Is there anything you want to tell the crowd?"

She'd played tremendously well, apparently, and excelled at something she had barely ever tried. Thousands of people stared down at her, radiating pure admiration towards her, all waiting on her merest pronouncement. Molly felt a swelling sensation within her, a kind of welling up. "Actually," she said, "I do gotta go pee. Thanks guys, see you whenever it is I play next."

◆

There was only one place to celebrate a tennis victory of course, and one way to thoroughly quench the adrenaline coursing through her veins from her physical activity and triumph. "With nutella again, please," she said. "And this time, could I have ten waffles? Thank you."

She was contemplating ordering a second batch when Ham walked past. She squealed and tried to hide some of her waffle plates under the table. Molly was sitting at the picture window on the café's front, looking out across the town square, and he saw her almost as soon as she saw him, which meant he almost certainly noticed her frantically thrusting six plates onto the seat of the chair across from her. Nevertheless, he walked in, moved the plates to another table, and sat down.

"This place," she said. "They sell a hell of a single waffle to a girl, but they really don't know how to bus a table."

The waiter chose this moment to stop by. "Madame, we can do another five waffles now, but if you do want the additional ten the chef will need to send out for more eggs."

"What? You beefwitted poltroon, I don't want any waffles!" Molly yelled. As the waiter walked off, she grabbed his wrist and whispered, "Just put the five in a bag and I'll come back for the rest later."

"I heard about your match," said Ham. "Nice work."

"Thank you. Apparently I won a golden shower."

"I think you mean set," he said. "Unless the prizes have gotten really strange here."

"Haha, you're so witty Ham," Molly said. "Would you like a coffee or anything?" she added, noticing the waiter had come back with a large parcel, which she hid deftly.

"Oh, I'm okay," he said. "I was just going for a walk if you want to come with?"

They wandered for hours around the town, talking of their lives and their dreams and their ambitions. Or so Molly assumed, anyway. Ham was so handsome she found it difficult paying attention to anything he actually said. However time passed quickly anyway, and they were just finishing their fifth complete circuit of the town when their perambulations were interrupted by a pitiful mewling coming from a nearby tree.

Molly peered up and saw a small coppery kitten caught in a high branch. Its fur was the same shade as the autumn leaves surrounding it, and it kept batting one oversized paw at the air, seemingly in the vain hope it would become solid enough to walk upon.

"Awww, we'll help you kitty," Molly said.

"I'll handle this," said Ham, and he took off his shirt and threw it into the tree. His torso was like an anatomist's sketch of ideal human musculature. Did he have good abs? Abs-olutely. His arms were sheathed in long smooth muscle and his shoulders were so broad that if they were in a movie from the forties Humphrey Bogart would be buying them a drink and then trying to sleep with at least one of them.

"Huh," said Ham. "I guess I just assumed that would have some kind of a net effect?"

"Slurwurble garffle narfle?" Molly said, then swallowed down her drool. "I mean, I guess it was a good attempt. Here, boost me up." He hefted her onto his shoulders and she enticed the kitty into her arms and also grabbed his shirt. He went to put it on again, but she said, "Actually the kitty was scared and might be cold. We should wrap it in your shirt, in case it goes into cat-iac arrest."

Unfortunately the kitty had an ID tag and they were able to deliver it home, after which Ham had to put his shirt back on.

◆

After the shirtless cat adventure, the sun was setting and Ham had to join his sister to stake out, as he kept putting it though Molly kept refusing to acknowledge the pun, the tennis centre for vampire activity. She was feeling tired and flustered, and so returned to the hotel room. Vampire Umpire was in the final stages of his byzantine and diabolical scheme.

"Hey Matt," he was saying as she entered the room. "It turned out Bruce didn't say you smell. He said you played *well*. It was just a bad phone line." There was a pause as Matt spoke, and then Vampire Umpire continued, "And I enjoyed speaking to you too. See you at the match and goodbye for now." He turned to Molly. "Hey, I hear you did great today!"

"Oh thanks! Yeah, I got to see Ham shirtless AND I ate a whole bunch of waffles. I tell you, the toilet is gonna regret meeting me tomorrow."

"I meant the tennis match. Only seven golden sets have ever been recorded in the history of tennis."

"Oh. Cool I guess."

Vampire Umpire laughed. "But I guess someone has more of a craving for the mouth-watering taste of Ham."

"Shut up! I do not!" Molly was blushing.

"You totally do! Someone wants to spit-roast some Ham." He paused. "Umm, actually that one got away from me a bit."

"Yeah, plus it's not like you aren't going weak at the knees for Ioana."

"Yes, but I suspect that's mainly because her perfume is fatal to me. Literally," he added, frowning.

"Mehhhhhh, I think that despite being technically dead, your heart races a little when she's around."

"Well I think you are like a curious Jewish child, and wanting some Ham inside you."

"Well I think your room temperature form is growing almost imperceptibly warm for her."

"I think probably we could do this all night," Vampire Umpire said, "and I have already delayed this match by ten hours."

"True, you should go. I'm just going to stay here and study my book again."

"Okay, let me know how season 5 turns out."

◆

Molly lay asleep, a discarded bowl of crisps fallen to spill on the floor below her bed, her laptop stalled on one of the later episodes of her TV show. The screen flickered a couple of times, then a grey bar scrolled slowly across, warping the images of the colourful sitcom characters into grey-fleshed ghouls with hollow spaces where there eyes once were. The screen fizzled and random pops and hisses burbled from the speakers. The laptop burned out.

In her dream, Molly wore a pale blue silk nightgown and her hair was tied in bows on either side of her head. She felt a tremendous cold all around her, as if a layer of ice were congealing around her and clinging to her body. Ahead of her, as if in a dark tunnel with only hazy light illuminating him, she thought she saw Ham. He beckoned her with one arm crooked towards her. "Come to me," he whispered, the words falling flat in the dead air yet somehow she heard.

She moved towards him, but her limbs lacked all energy and it took all her will to take each step. She stumbled towards him, on legs that felt unlike her own. Ahead of him a terrible clanging tolled slowly, like a deep bell ringing some terrible call. Her body too felt different, a little heavier in the torso, less strength in her arms.

"There's something I must show you," he said. He seemed to grow ever more distant, and she chased him, but it was as if her every effort granted impetus to his movements instead of her own. The bell boomed again. She tumbled forwards and woke.

She was in the hall, standing near the huge window that looked out to the river several hundred feet below. The catch was loose and the wind tore through the window slamming it open and shut with a furious clanging. A gust blasted the window open and it rebounded hard from the wall. Still woozy from the dream and the almost myoclonic jerk with which she had awoken, Molly was off-balance and almost falling anyway, when the edge caught her square on the temple. Disoriented, battered, she reeled forward and fell through the pane and tumbled down through the night.

Chapter Five

Vampire Umpire leaned forward in his umpiring chair and shook each players' hand as they walked up to him. "Well played," he told both men.

"Nice umpiring," Matt said. "And not just because I won. Your calls were as smooth and seamless as a freshly shaved back."

"Thank you," said Vampire Umpire. "That was beautifully phrased."

He slipped out of the tennis centre quietly, leaving the players to do their interviews and enjoy the attentions of the crowd. The night air was wrapped in the orange, gossamer light of the nearby town, and to Vampire Umpire it seemed to bathe his body in warmth. He recalled few times in life when he had been happier: he was pursuing his dream and he had made a good new friend.

In the bushes nearby, Ham and Jean were crouched, camouflage make up smeared inexpertly across their faces. He waved at them politely, and Jean scowled and scuttled further back into the shrub in which she hid, but Ham waved and came over. "Hi Vampire Umpire," he said.

"Hey Ham. Still out vampire hunting?"

"Yeah. Jean and I were planning to follow the players home."

"For… sexual reasons?"

"Oh god no. To see if a vampire attacks one of them." He frowned. "But actually maybe the vampire just hates umpires! Gosh Vampire Umpire, what if you are the next one the vampire attacks?"

"Oh, I'm sure I'll be fine. I run really fast."

"No, I'd better walk you home. Hey Jean! Jean! JEAN!"

Jean's face appeared in the bush, red and angry. "God dammit, Ham, this is supposed to be a covert operation. What part of covert do you feel is screaming my name into the night like a deranged maniac who loves me?"

"Oh Jean," Vampire Umpire said. "You're a fine person: just because someone loves you doesn't mean they are insane."

"I'm talking to my brother," Jean said, scowling. "Do you remember any of our stealth training as children?"

"What training?" Ham said, a gormless look on his face.

"You know, when Dad would make us hide, then count to one hundred, then seek us out? And how if he found us, we'd only get one dessert each instead of two?"

"Oh yeah, sorry. But I'm going to just walk Vampire Umpire home and then I'll meet you at the waffle house."

"NOT the waffle house. Assembly point alpha."

"But we're still getting waffles, right?"

"Maybe, the chef told me someone ate them out of stock earlier."

♦

Vampire Umpire and Ham walked towards the hotel. "Monster hunter is an interesting profession," Vampire Umpire said. "How did you get started in it?"

"Oh it was when we were kids, I guess," Ham said. "I think I was around five, and I remember my parents fighting all the time. My mom never told me why, but one night Dad came into me and Jean's bedroom and he told us he had to leave to fight the forces of darkness."

"He did? Why?"

"He said Mom never wanted him to tell us, but the world was full of monsters and he was the Slayer, a man born into the world to protect humanity from the demons that prey on it."

"That sounds a lot like the plot of Buff…"

"Buffy the Vampire Slayer, yeah. But he explained later that they had based that show on stories of his life from before he had us."

"So he…?"

"Well, he was pretty drunk that night, which he told us was to protect him from the demon Bibulous, who must be super-powerful because me and Jean can find no mention of It in any of our grimoires. But he still was brave enough to drive off into the night to go fight some monsters that very night."

"I… see."

"Yeah. It was a hard life, and he ended up living in a trailer park with some woman who he accidentally got pregnant while seeking romantic comfort after a tough case, as paranormal investigators often do. It's in the manual my Dad wrote, which I'd show you but it was all on some napkins that I had an accident with."

"And how old is your half sibling?" Vampire Umpire asked.

"Oh, because of a time paradox, Gina is actually midway between me and Jean in age," Ham said.

"Your life is one of great tragedy," Vampire Umpire said. "Do you never wonder…" Far in the distance his vampire eyes saw the oscillations of the hotel window, and he saw Molly plunge out. He raced with all his speed towards the hotel and dived into the ravine mere milliseconds after Molly fell into it. He cradled her in his arms, cushioning the force of the fall, and swept upwards toward the safety of the ground.

"Nice catch," she said. "Thank you."

"You're more than welcome," he said.

Ham ran up to them, breathless and panting. "Wow... you... sure... can... run... fast," he said.

"Wow," whispered Molly. "He looks so good all sweaty."

"Keep it in your pants, at least while I'm here," Vampire Umpire whispered back.

Ham had caught his breath and now the only evidence of his sprint was a faint almost post-coital blush on his cheeks and some sweat on his brow that Molly was halfway considering claiming she needed to lick off as the fall had left her dehydrated. "Let's get you inside so you can lie down," he said.

"That's pretty forward, but maybe we can go to your place?" she said. "I'm not going back into that hotel room: it's haunted."

Her second sentence seemed to distract them from their first. They asked the expected follow up questions and she told them about the weird happenings on the first night, and how tonight she had felt possessed.

"We need to go in and confront the spirit," Ham said.

"Nuh uh," Molly said. "I'm afraid of this ghost."

"You seem to have some connection to it," he said, "and we need to lay it to rest."

"He might be right," Vampire Umpire said. "I have some experience fighting ghosts." Later, when Molly confronted him about this alleged experience, he admitted that it consisted entirely of an almost crippling Ms. Pac-Man addiction in the late eighties.

When they walked into the bedroom, Ham started crawling around, sniffing the sheets and the corners of the ceiling. "I don't smell any brimstone," he said. "But all my equipment is in the car. I'm going to have to go and get some. Vampire Umpire, don't leave her alone okay?" He placed a delicate-fingered, smooth-fleshed hand on Molly's shoulder and she moaned.

"That was a fear moan," she said, playing hard to get. "I'm playing hard to get," she added, ill-advisedly.

Ham stared at her sadly. "You don't need to worry. The ghost isn't going to *get* you while me and Vampire Umpire are here." Once he left, Vampire Umpire sat on the bed and rubbed the back of his neck.

"No offence to your love interest," he said, "but I wonder if we might be better solving this ourselves."

"But how?" Molly said. "How do we fight a ghost?"

"Well, ghosts are simply spirits who remain because of some unfinished business," he began.

"Yeah, unfinished like *dying*," Molly said.

"Dying is what gives our lives meaning," the immortal vampire said. "It's the period at the end of the sentence. Without death, none of the decisions we make have any consequence; it's not meaningful to spend your life doing one thing if you can spend another lifetime doing another."

"So that's why not every dead person becomes a ghost?"

"Yes. It needs to be a life lost aching for some thing impossible to attain in the world of the dead."

"Like a Five Guys burger?"

"I mean, I've never heard of a ghost being exorcised by the world's finest burger, but pretty much."

Molly sat beside him on the bed and started kicking her legs idly back and forth. "I guess, I mean… last night the ghost just watched sitcoms with me. And I think stole all of my popcorn."

Vampire Umpire knew that ghosts could never eat, but he also knew that sometimes people needed their dignity. "That greedy bastard," he said.

"And when I fell out of the window, actually I was just in the hall. The window hit me, but after I woke."

"So something in the hall, then?"

They stepped out into the corridor. Molly turned on the flashlight on her phone and began shining it over the walls.

Vampire Umpire simply looked around, straining his vampire senses to the full.

"There's something strange and stinky here," Molly said. Vampire Umpire walked over.

"Yeah, that's a cigarette butt," Vampire Umpire said. "But it is stinky and disgusting."

"Maybe the ghost hates smokers as much as we do?"

"Possible, but unlikely. Hold on," he said. He walked over to the window and closed the catch properly. Then he knelt down and began picking at the corner of the wallpaper.

"Noice," Molly said. "Doing a little vandalism. You so gangsta, Vampie U."

"Not quite." He peeled the paper entirely off the wall, like a scab from a wound. Underneath, the greying old woodwork was marred by a huge white circle of slightly fresher plaster.

"In my dream," Molly began, "I was being enclosed by someone."

"Yes," said Vampire Umpire. He pulled his fist back to punch through the plaster but Molly stopped him.

"No, I want to," she said. She picked a fire extinguisher off the wall from further down the corridor and held it in both hands. She slammed the base into the plaster, across which a crack bigger than one would find on a fat man's ass began to spread. A few more blows and the hall had filled with disturbed guests, who Vampire Umpire restrained with his usual exquisite politeness, and a fine mist of plaster dust. Molly shone her torch into the hole.

A mummified face leered back at her, eyeless and lipless. The drying out of the facial muscles had contorted the visage into the semblance of a grin. A veil lay on the ground beside the corpse, who it seemed was garbed in a wedding dress. The corpse reached for Molly, and she stepped back, screaming.

Vampire Umpire held her. "It just fell forward," he said. "The disturbance must have knocked it over."

"Yeah," said Molly. And yet... The corpse's arm now poked through the wall, and in the tight grey coil of its hand, which resembled nothing more than a slab of petrified wood riddled with small fractures, something glimmered in the hall lights. "What is that?" she said.

Vampire Umpire gently uncurled the fingers, which released with a small popping sound that reminded Molly of the wishbone of a chicken cracking. "A name badge," he said.

♦

Molly and Vampire Umpire stood in front of the concierge desk. "I'm sorry," Molly said, "but I'm afraid we did some damage to your wall."

"In your room, I presume?" the concierge said. "Well, it is something to be young and in love."

"Not the room," Vampire Umpire said. "The hall."

The concierge went pale. "The hall?"

"Yes," said Molly. "It is something to be young and in love," she continued. "Like in this letter I found. A young bride wrote it on her wedding day, to the first boyfriend she had and sadly never grew to love. Even though she'd told him truly how she felt, he refused to accept she loved the man she was marrying."

"Apparently she visited him on the morning of her wedding, to give him the letter," Vampire Umpire continued. "And I think he never let her deliver it."

The concierge was trembling. "She wrote me a letter?" he asked, each word quavering out more uncertainly than the last.

"You took her somewhere private, didn't you?" Molly asked. "And you probably tried to touch her, and she tried to run, and you fought, and you killed her."

"I never meant…"

"Whatever," Molly said. She slapped his old nametag down on the desk. "The police are coming and this and the body will be enough to convict you." She rolled up her sleeves. "Oh, and since you're old, I'm doing this instead of him."

"Doing what?" the concierge began to say before her fist smashed hard into his face.

"And for the record," Vampire Umpire said, "I'm stronger because of reasons to do with our inherent natures, not because I'm a man and she's a woman."

◆

Molly fell asleep that night while finishing the last episode of the fourth season of Seinfeld. Vampire Umpire pulled the sheet over her gently, and he wondered briefly if he was imagining the faint impression of a hand that seemed to caress her cheek softly before dissipating into the air.

Her dreams that night were sweet and peaceful, and she woke feeling refreshed and pure.

Chapter Six

Tyrone Ennis met them both outside the courts after the final. "Congratulations on your latest victory," he said, shaking Molly's hand with both of his, which enclosed her slender fingers the way gristly pork encloses the egg in a scotch egg.

"Thank you," Molly said. "I really wonder if I'm going to still play tennis if I ever lose a match. I mean almost certainly not, but that'll probably never even happen."

"Exactly," said Vampire Umpire. "It's the victory, not how the game is played."

Tyrone Ennis frowned slightly and said, "Just don't say any of that to the press, okay? Are you going to the closing celebration tonight?"

"Please," said Molly. "Free food and free drink and you have to ask?"

Tyrone laughed. "I only wish I could join you. Sadly I was at a business lunch earlier and I had the fish and I think it's made me ill."

"That sounds like food poissoning," said Vampire Umpire and raised one eyebrow. Like someone having their first sexual experience, he held it for several seconds but his partners were unimpressed. Sadly neither Tyrone Ennis nor Molly seemed to get the joke.

"That's pretty insensitive," Tyrone said, while simultaneously Molly was saying, "It's pronounced 'poisoning', Dumbpire Umpire."

There was, Vampire Umpire realised, a time and a place for ingenious bilingual verbal word-play, and he suspected it was actually a century ago. "I apologise," he said.

"Anyway," said Tyrone. "I'm going to go back to the hotel and rest. I hope you guys do as well tonight as you did in the tournament, Molly."

He wandered off, occasionally pausing to vomit as decorously as possible into nearby bins, and Molly said, "What do you think he meant by that?"

"I have no clue," said Vampire Umpire. "Maybe he just hopes you demolish the buffet as thoroughly as you do your opposition?"

◆

The answer became clear though when they entered the banquet hall. A large sign across the stage read AUSTRIAN TENNIS CHAMPIONSHIP CELEBRATION AND RAP BATTLE. "Rap battle?" Molly said, turning almost as pale as Vampire Umpire.

"I'm sure you won't have to rap," Vampire Umpire reassured her.

The public address system crackled to life. "All players must rap. Players should register for the rap battle to receive their dinner plates."

"You mean…" Molly said.

"I'm afraid so: unless you rap, I don't think you get any dinner."

"Just like at an orphanage," she said, sadly.

The registration table was a small desk with a green felt cloth covering it. A woman sat behind it, next to a small stack of large white dinner plates. As they walked up, Molly confessed something shocking to Vampire Umpire. "I can't rap at all," she said. The woman at the desk overheard her and said, "It is acceptable to enter as a duo or trio, Ms. Durand. Many players, having devoted their lives entirely to tennis, have correspondingly neglected to similarly develop their flow and rhyme freshness." She shook her head. "And yet is it not an important thing to live as full a life as one can?"

"Well that seems weirdly judgemental," Molly said. "There are other talents besides tennis and rap, you know."

"So what skills do you possess?" the woman asked.

Molly was a woman of immense talents. She was an eloquent and engaging writer, hilarious, could cook well and bake beautifully, was socially adept and a charming conversationalist, and possessed numerous other skills. Sadly her mind now went blank, and all she said was, "I can have my feelings hurt," and she hunched over about to cry.

"Could I enter on a team with Ms. Durand?" Vampire Umpire asked, placing a consoling arm around her shoulders to still the incipient tears.

"You're not a player, so it is allowed," she said. "However you are the last to regiser so…"

Molly immediately interrupted her, "So all the food is gone from the buffet?"

"No, there is still plenty of food." Molly sighed and relaxed immediately. "But you two will be the last to perform, and you're going on right after Jeb Moslius, who always puts on the most extraordinary show."

"But there's plenty of food, right?" asked Molly.

◆

Molly's plate was piled to cornucopian proportions with every kind of food. She had insisted that Vampire Umpire apportion his plate similarly, even though he would eat none of it, so that she could have, in her words, "double buffet without double the walking." There was every delicious kind of food represented: rare steak in a peppercorn sauce; skewers of chicken teriyaki so succulent the meat almost peeled off the stick as it was raised from plate to mouth; finely prepared spaghetti with a rich tomato sauce so thick it practically clotted one's arteries just looking at it and cheese melting in long strings that were thick enough to bind Jörmungandr itself.

"I need all of that inside me," Molly said with a kind of maddened lust. (There will be no further erotic writing in this novel, the reader should be aware. That will follow in the sequel, which is provisionally titled 'A Bone-fortunate Series of Events'.)

"Do you not want to prepare for the rap battle even at all?"

"Mmmmmff, mffff, snrrrr, grrrarg," said Molly.

"I... see."

She swallowed down a good glug of wine. "If you say you can rap, you can rap," she said. "So it will probably be fine."

"Okay then. Oh, sorry," Molly was gesturing with large sweeping motions of her arm, as if pulling a portly man into a hug or miming the enclosure of land that destroyed England's peasant classes, that she wished him to pass over her plate. It now belonged to her, as did the portly man who was hugged by her, or the rich people the enclosed farming pastures.

"I guess I will just freestyle it," Vampire Umpire said, thoughtfully.

♦

The crowd of fans and tennis players left the tables and began to drift towards the stage, slowly at first but ever more rapidly, like stars being pulled in to orbit a black hole. The host and judge of the rap battle eventually climbed onto the stage. "Good evening," he said. "I'm Phife Dawg and I am pleased to judge this battle of rhyming tennis titans." The man was white (Phife Dawg had in life traditionally appeared to be a black man) and was for some reason wearing a fake beard, even though underneath was visible the man's actual beard.

"But isn't Phife Dawg dead?" a number of people in the crowd asked each other.

On stage, Phife Dawg continued, "If there is anything I enjoy more than," he pulled a piece of paper from his pocket and consulted it, "moneys and hos," he read, "it is the noble sport of tennis."

Molly said, "Yeah, Phife Dawg died of diabetes this year. I remember because I know a diabetic and I keep hoping he goes the same way but for some reason he keeps clinging to life like a hideous limpet clings to a boat that would be better off without it."

"Well, some people can be quite… shellfish," Vampire Umpire said, and Molly punched him hard in the arm.

"Who are you actually?" Molly shouted.

"Oh fine!" Phife Dawg pulled off his beard and underneath was Tyrone Ennis. The crowd, uniformly having penetrated the deception, singularly refused to gasp in shock.

"But Phife Dawg didn't even have a beard!" Molly shouted.

"I needed a disguise!"

"The first part of disguising yourself as a man with no beard isn't to wear a fake beard over your actual beard," Vampire Umpire, a master of the art of disguise, pointed out.

"Okay, okay, fine," Tyrone Ennis said. "The truth is Phife Dawg was the only rapper who liked tennis and when he died this year I could find no-one to judge the rap contest. So, despite getting food poisoning, I decided to use my acting skills to put on a ruse, which a few sharp-eyed spectators have admittedly seen through."

"We all knew straight away," Molly informed him.

"Literally everyone," Vampire Umpire clarified.

"Fine okay. It was intended as a loving tribute to a titan of the music industry."

"And now you're calling him fat? Duuuuude. The guy was diabetic," said Molly.

"Let's start the show!" Tyrone Ennis shouted.

The first contestant happened to be Matt Berninger. He got on stage accompanied by four people with instruments: two twin brothers with guitars and a bassist and drummer. The band started playing a sweet simple song with a beautiful melody, and Matt started singing in a delicate, elegant baritone:

We expected something,
Something better than before.
We expected something more.

Do you really think that you can put it in a safe
Behind a painting lock it up and leave?
Walk away now, and you're going to start a war.

Whatever went away, I'll get it over now
I'll get money, I'll get funny again.
Whatever we-

The power to the band's amps was cut abruptly, and Tyrone Ennis walked onto the stage going, "No, no," and making chopping gestures across his throat with his hand.

The crowd, which had been slowly moved into dancing along to the song, shouted a generalised disapproval and Tyrone Ennis continued, "I'm sorry but that is a song, not a rap song." The crowd settled down pretty fast – as good as the song had been, it wasn't rap and that meant it wasn't appropriate to perform at a rap battle. So while they might have enjoyed it, they respected Tyrone Ennis' decision to stop the performance and disqualify Matt. "I'm sorry Matt," he said, "but this means you have to pay for your dinner."

"Goddammit," said Matt. "What do I owe you?"

"It's about forty pounds," Tyrone Ennis said.

Matt searched through his wallet. "I only have thirty two," he said.

"Oh, I have 10," said Vampire Umpire.

"And here's two change," said Tyrone Ennis, handing the coin to Vampire Umpire.

"Actually," Matt said, "if you give me the two pounds, then I can just get ten and give that to Vampire Umpire later."

"I'm fine with that," said Vampire Umpire. "I don't really like coins anyway." Sadly, as none of the crowd knew he was a vampire, no-one got this clever reference, and even in a novel, where someone has time to appreciate every nuance of the language it is probably the kind of remark that a clever writer would flag up in some obvious way.

The matter settled, the night proceeded. The next few performers were weak, and by the end of the night the crowd's opinion seemed generally settled that the best performance had been by Bruce Sprungfeld. He had stepped onto the stage and, against a standard backing track provided by Tyrone Ennis' sound crew, had delivered the following tight verse:

I said a rap, rap, rappity rap
Rap rap rappity rap.
I said a rap, rap, rappity rap
Rap rap rappity rap.

This had gone on for two encores, and many of the audience felt that it had been the finest rap anyone had ever performed. Now however, only two performances remained. Jebediah Moslius walked onto the stage and grabbed the microphone from the stand. "I'm the number one tennis player in the world," he shouted, ignoring the shout of "for now" from some not so random person in the audience. "And me and my partner are also the number one rappers in the world. Please welcome to the stage... Kanye West."

Kanye West strode out from stage right, dressed in a potato sack into which he had artfully torn several rips. He had painted his naked legs blue, which was basically explained by a sign that read: "Yo if Levi don't want to let me design their jeans, I'll show them jeans are just a social construct." Sadly, the density of information was too great and the sign was illegible to anyone either not on the stage or a vampire.

A weird rhythmic track started playing, with snare drums blended into a weird mix of short melodic passages chopped into almost incoherence and some sampled screaming. Somewhere within there was a beat, and Kanye began to rap over it:

Everybody denying it but y'all know I'm a genius.
No I ain't joking I totally mean this.
I say dope things in my songs
And I bang hot bitches all wearing thongs
Slip em to the side and I put in my penis
Slop it all around and make 'em scream yes.
And if I have a good time I unleash my cream jets.
I don't care who you is you gonna be my lady
I don't like condoms so you'll have my baby.
I got more white stuff to go around than snow on a mountain
I don't call it a dick - I've got a penis fountain.
If you're a lady you know we be having sex
I'll put it in your vag then put it in your necks
My aim's not great so me oh my
There is a good chance I'm gonna spunk in your eye.
If you in the kitchen I'll spunk in your pie.

Girl you gotta boyfriend? I'll spunk in your guy.

SPPPPPUUUUUUUNNNNNNNKKKKKK.

"Now you gotta thank me," Kanye said, "for giving you the greatest moment of your lives."

"Thank us both," Moslius added, even though his contribution to the… song had been just standing behind Kanye and occasionally pointing at him with both index fingers and winking.

The general feeling of the crowd was that they had no clue if what they had heard had been good or not, but they were aware that Kanye West was a very popular musician, so they assumed it must have been pretty solid. They applauded until Tyrone Ennis came to the stage. "I guess that's probably the winning entry," he said. "But first we have our last performance: Molly Durand and her crew, Vampire Umpire."

In the wings, Jebediah Moslius booed loudly, and Molly flipped him off as she walked out. She sat down at the piano and cracked her fingers once. Vampire Umpire walked up to the microphone. It was flecked with what, in the best case scenario, he hoped was Kanye's spit. He took a white silk handkerchief from his pocket, wiped the mic clean and then handed the handkerchief to a stagehand in the wings, asking him to throw it out. "Just play me something with a solid 16 bars and a nice even beat, please," he said to Molly.

She thought for a moment and then began to play a complex interlocking pair of melodies. One part was three bars long, one five, and the variation in their combination had an almost hypnotically lovely affect.

Vampire Umpire let it ride for a few bars before he started to rap:

Before I was a rapper I was a street poet
Erase the beat my words still flow. It
Used to be rappers spat about more than just sex
And now they're fat and bores riding private jets
Around with their wives who have about as much talent.
And if they weren't famous they couldn't pay the rent
On a single room in a discarded farmhouse
With nothing in the cupboards but a hungry mouse,
Yet somehow they're in penthouses in New York City,
Lined with platinum discs though their songs are shitty.
I've been learning rhyming since the days of Dante,
Writing words and timings of exquisite beauty.
When I write a verse I think it is a crime if I can't haunt

You like a curse and slink a triple rhyme while I flaunt

My skills by really rhyming four in a line

And then you count back and you know I did fine.

Rapping at its best is a poem telling truths

In words of beauty geared to the ear of youths,

Not mindlessly listing your misogynistic nonsense,

Uttering nothing but your solipsistic lack of conscience.

He dropped the mic and walked off the stage. The crowd went wild. In the wings, Kanye placed a hand on his chest. "You're right man," Kanye said. "I need to change."

"Just do your best," Vampire Umpire said. He clasped Kanye's hand for a moment, and the lesser rapper walked off, shoulders slumped.

On stage, Tyrone Ennis was walking back and forth rubbing his forehead free of sweat. "Oh my god, oh my god," he was saying into the mic. The crowd was still going crazy. Tyrone Ennis took Molly's hand and raised it high in the air. "Ladies and gentleman do you deny this is the winner of the rap battle?" he shouted.

"We love you!" the crowd shouted at her.

"Is she the winner?"

"She's the winner," they roared back in perfect unison.

"Ladies and gentleman, Molly Durand, winner of the Austrian Tennis Championship also wins the RAPPPPP BATTTLE."

Back stage, Vampire Umpire heard Jeb Moslius say, "This is bullshit" and kick open the stage door and storm out, but that was lost to everyone else in the ceaseless, overwhelming adulation of the crowd, and their chant of "Molly MOLLY MOLLY! MOLLY!!"

Chapter Seven

The rap battle was followed by a dance, as was the tradition of the form. Admittedly, in the hallowed days of Biggie and Tupac, it had technically been more a cotillion than a dance that followed, but time, like those overrated rappers, had passed since then. A small string quartet was brought up to the stage and they played while the tennisers and the staff and their guests transcribed elegant arabesques on the floor below.

Vampire Umpire and Molly danced the first dance, a waltz, together. "Do you know how to dance?" he asked her.

"You tell me," she said, and started bobbing up and down from the knees. She cast an imaginary lasso around Vampire Umpire and mimed reeling him towards her.

"So no?"

"Well, not old timey dances," she complained.

"Just follow me, and for once let me lead, okay?" He placed her hand on his shoulder and rested his lightly just above her hip, and he clasped her hand in his. It felt cool and dry, like a well deodorised armpit, and even more pleasant than that sounds. He led her onto the dance floor and they glided around the chamber like a pen in a Spirograph: regularly and with beautiful precision.

"Thanks for your help winning the rap battle," she said. "I really didn't want to pay for my dinner."

"I barely did a thing," he said, twirling her under his arm. She caught a zephyr of his scent, clean and pleasant as a forest in the cool of spring. She stumbled slightly, but he turned it into a neat dip, and pulled her against him again. "It is like the painter thanking the canvas for existing."

"I guess," Molly said. "I *did* do most of the work." He spun her around a wide, seemingly slow spiral that somehow ended with her feet lifting into the air with the speed of it, and for a moment it was as if she were flying. "I'm maybe going to enter and win some more rap battles."

"That's a good idea," he said.

"But you have to come on stage with me," she said. "Y'know. For luck."

"Always," he said.

The song had ended, and somehow Vampire Umpire had contrived it so that they were back at their seats. He let go of her hands but didn't step back. Her mouth felt dry. "Could you get me a drink?" she asked him.

"Of course," he said and headed off to the bar. Moments after he left, as if the vampire's absence had been awaited, Ham walked up to her.

"Hey," he said. "That was some good rapping earlier. I love rap and I gotta say, that was one of the best rap songs ever rapped, in my opinion."

"Thanks," she said. "I'd literally never rapped before but I think I'm just naturally more talented than everyone else, like an X-Man."

"An X-Man?"

"You know, Homo sapiens superior?"

"Oh," he said and the smile flushed off his face like a snot rag down a toilet. "I didn't know you were gay."

"Ha, no, like how you're a homo sapien."

"Hey, sure, maybe I did some stuff with a friend in high school but that was just experimentation and he shouldn't be telling anyone about it," Ham said, flustered.

"No," she said, though her loins could stand to hear more about this handsome man getting it on with another, in imagination at least, equally handsome man. As she believed the old saying went, after all, two penises were better than one. "Homo sapiens is the entire human species."

"Ah, right," Ham said. "I guess that will help with the overpopulation I have been hearing about at least."

"Do you want to dance?" she asked, sensing that this conversation was an ouroboros with no good end.

"Of course," he said. He grabbed her hand and they walked out onto the floor.

◆

Vampire Umpire had not taken long to get Molly's drink. Her tastes were, like Henry the Eighth's with women, unfortunately catholic, so nearly any drink would do. He decided she would want something refreshing though, after their dance, and so got her a bottle of Tiger beer. One of the best things about being a vampire was using your hypnotic powers to get served quickly at bars. He merely stepped up, mesmerised the bartender and got the beer. Of course it was tricky sometimes getting the bartender to accept payment, but at the worst he used his vampire speed to plant the money secretly in some pocket of their clothing. The invention of pockets (by Guillermo de Pocket, in 1784) had essentially perfected bar-bibulosity for the impatient but ethical vampire.

As he walked back across the dance floor towards Molly, elegantly sidestepping terpsichorean couples, he saw that she was talking to Ham, and he smiled gently. From her body language, he saw that things were progressing quite effectively there. One thing Molly had taught him during their friendship was the importance of something people in the modern world called the "Bro Code," which here specified that his role as Molly's "bro" was not to get in the way of her "slipping the bone train into the metaphorical station" of her chosen "ho," who in this case was Ham. He decided to give them the requisite space.

He stepped off subtly towards the side of the room, where he saw Ioana sitting alone and disconsolate at a table. Her phone sat out on the tableclock, and she kept checking it and then almost throwing it down with a force that would probably have made it explode if it had been manufactured by Samsung. "May I join you?" he asked. She gestured at a chair and he sat down. As always, her garlic scent made him feel light-headed. "Are you having a nice evening?"

"No," she said. "Jeb has just abandoned me here and he's not replying to my messages."

"Ah well," said Vampire Umpire. "Perhaps a drink will help?" He placed the beer on the table, close to her hand but he was careful not to touch her.

She slurped a mouthful out. "Thanks," she said.

"The music is pleasant, the beer is cold, and all around people dance with such joy that you can almost feel the happiness warm the room," he said. "So perhaps your night is imperfect, but it doesn't have to be a total loss."

♦

If they had been keeping a tally, Ham and Molly had probably stomped on each other's feet roughly equally, but as he was essentially a hulking behemoth of muscle and easily four times her weight she felt that overall she was the aggrieved party. The main casualties, as in a war, were the innocent bystanders, however. Like a faulty iPod, neither Ham nor Molly seemed to be able to remain in sync, and they regularly collided with other dancers, sending wavelets of chaotic motion rippling through the dancers, like a clumsy rock thrown into a previously still pond.

"So what do your parents do now?" Molly asked, accidentally ramming her elbow hard into the crotch of a male dancer behind her. Over the music and the man's groans, she couldn't hear his answer, but she went with "Oh cool!", which due to their translation to the far end of the hall, away from the band, became more audible.

"I… *guess* it's cool being an orphan," Ham said thoughtfully.

Eeeep, Molly thought. "Well I just mean, it must be nice being like Harry Potter or Bruce Wayne."

"Or that guy who always wants more food?"

"Oliver Twist?"

"No, I think it's," Ham's handsome brow furrowed in thought, and his musculature was so strong that she could hear the creak of his mighty face muscles, "Yeah. It's Hannibal Lecter."

"Oh right, he's quite old so he probably is an orphan," said Molly. Ham nodded vigorously, inadvertently head-butting someone behind him.

She felt his fingers stroke the line of the side of her hip, and a shiver rolled down her spine. She danced in close against him, swaying her arms around. She didn't notice the woman ducking to avoid her inadvertent swing, nor feel the slap of her fingers volleying the woman's tiara across the room where it knocked over a large glass of wine so red it looked as purple as one of Prince's codpieces. The wine spilled a great dark stain over the white silk tablecloth, like arterial spray against fresh snow. But Molly's consciousness was lost in the glow of Ham's eyes.

♦

The phone vibrated and lit up on the table. By natural reaction, Vampire Umpire read the message:

"I'm at the hotel, ffs. I'm getting a massage after my match today, I'll be an hour. Bring that ass around about 11, Dummy."

Ioana picked her phone off the table, read the message and tapped out a long reply. She thought for a moment, then deleted it and put in a shorter message. Vampire Umpire saw it read "K, love you, Ioana xxx".

"He calls you Dummy?" Vampire Umpire asked.

"It is a pet name," Ioana said. "My surname is Dumitrescu, and he said that was 'Too much effort to say'," she laughed a merry little trill of a laugh, "so he calls me Dumi instead."

Vampire Umpire considered pointing out the actual meaning of her 'pet name,' but decided it was not his place to intervene. Especially as now the message was received, Ioana seemed slightly happier.

"Have you ever lived in Romania?" she asked him. "I hear hints of my country in your accent sometimes."

"I did briefly, many ce... cycles of the moon ago," he said, hoping she didn't notice his verbal stumble. "In some ways I was born there."

"You were? Where?"

"A fairly isolated castle around some farmland near Dealul Mitropoliei," he said.

"But that is part of Bucharest," she said. "It has been for hundreds of years."

"Sorry, I misspoke," he said. "I do not speak English with any degree of either facility or felicity, I'm afraid. I meant, how you say, a suburb?" He had long ago learned that if you threw in the phrase 'how you say' in any language, a native speaker would let you feel get away with anything, feeling confident in their superiority.

"That's right," she said.

"But I moved away fairly soon after," he said. For several reasons he had had no desire to return to Bucharest and now he hadn't enough knowledge to answer any follow-on questions she might have safely.

"I feel like dancing," she said. "Will you dance with me?" She held out her hand, off which Vampire Umpire could smell the scent of garlic so strongly it seemed to be radiating in pulsing, visible waves.

"While it is…" he began to say, when he noticed a waiter passing. The waiter wore white gloves, and Vampire Umpire called him over. "Could I please borrow those?" he said.

Safely covered by the gloves, he led Ioana out onto the dance floor.

◆

It had been a clumsy excuse, but when Ham asked Molly if she wanted to go out to his car to see the stars, because his windshield was "really really clean" she had accepted readily. Now they sat next to each other on the front seats, looking up fruitlessly.

"I guess I forgot about light pollution," Ham said. They stared up into a night sky turned sodium yellow, in which no stars were visible and even the moon was overwhelmed.

"Still, the seats are really comfortable," Molly said. "Like, neato!" She bounced up and down on the seat merrily.

"Oh, could you not?" Ham said. "That's Jean's seat and she gets really picky about the settings."

"I mean, I'm not changing the settings."

"No but what if you rock something loose?"

"Uh, okay. I guess that's fair."

They sat in silence for a couple of minutes, and eventually Ham took her hand in his and held it. His grip was tight and hot. He pulled her towards him and she felt his plump lips mash against hers, and felt his tongue press wet between her lips and enter her mouth.

◆

Ioana had Vampire Umpire dance three or four dances with her, he did not particularly pay attention. After each she would check her phone, then they would dance again. Underneath the garlic, the scent of her body Vampire Umpire could detect was slightly more pleasant – faint traces of verbena seemed to be the main note. Their conversation flowed in small phrases between louder passages of the music and was stilted by necessity of that but also pleasant.

After their last dance, she gathered her things from the table. "I must go to see Jeb now," she said. She kissed Vampire Umpire once on each cheek, and took his still gloved hands. "I had a lot of fun tonight," she said, and for a moment her eyes met his and dwelled there thoughtfully, and then she left. It was fortunate, as his face began to sizzle and scorch, leaving the faint imprint of her lips burned into his cheeks. She *really* hefts that scent on, he thought.

He walked back to his and Molly's table and was considering his next move, when Molly walked back in, carrying her jacket over her shoulder flippantly.

"You're back?" he asked. "I thought I saw you leave with Ham."

"Oh," she said. "You saw that?" He nodded. "Yeah, he uh wanted me to show him how um car mud flaps work."

"Not your best lie," Vampire Umpire said.

"I mean that's fair. I think my strengths are in other areas."

"They do," he said. "So, do you want to talk about it?"

"Eh," she said. "Well we went to his car and he kissed me and it wasn't great."

"Oh, don't let that put you off. You can teach him to kiss better."

"I mean, maybe but then, well…"

"What?" asked Vampire Umpire.

"Well he kind of, well."

"This is sex related, isn't it?"

"He took it out," she said. "His penis, I mean."

"Ah, that is a bit forward," Vampire Umpire said.

"Oh no doubt," she said. "But the main problem was it looked exactly like a half-sucked lime tic tac." She paused for a moment then added, "In size *and* colour."

"I see," said Vampire Umpire. "So then that's over."

"YUP," she said.

"Come on," he said. "I'll take you to get some ice cream."

"That would be nice," she said.

"Just no mint choc chip," he added, and she punched his arm.

Chapter Eight

Molly and Vampire Umpire were packing up their hotel room when the knock came at the door. Vampire Umpire was playing Beyoncé's Lemonade, over and over, having become obsessed with it recently, and for a moment they mistook the knock for percussion.

"Was that a knock or drums?" Molly asked.

"I'm not sure," Vampire Umpire said. The sound came again and he realised that the sloppy timing of the knocking would never have passed muster in the recording studio while a perfectionist like Ms. Knowles was working. "The sloppy timing of that knocking would never have passed muster in the recording studio while a perfectionist like Ms. Knowles was working," he said.

"Ms. Knowles?"

"Yes."

"You know she's married to Jay-Z, right? So she's actually *Mrs. Carter.*"

"I refuse to accept any marriage as valid when it occurs between a luminous being like Beyonce and a hideous monster like Jason 'Jay-Z' Zedmore," Vampire Umpire said.

"Yeah, I don't think that's his actual name," she said.

"Pretty sure it is," he said. The knocking came again, a little louder, as if the person outside the door had heard their lengthy conversation and wished to remind them that the knocking had served a purpose other than stimulating a fascinating discussion.

Vampire Umpire opened the door. "Hi Ham," he said. "Are you here to see Molly?"

"Yeah," Ham said. "I was wanting to talk to her."

"Of course. I'll give you privacy."

"No, we need to pack," Molly said. In the background, the song All Night began playing, the neat little bass line walk around slowly being accompanied by the slinking strings line. "So just keep working and don't make a lot of ruckus."

Vampire Umpire was about to add, "Isn't that what you say during oral sex," but decided this wasn't the time.

Ham moved over to Molly and said to her, placing his hand on her shoulder, "I was really wondering if we could go out on a date." He whispered the words almost, clearly uncomfortable asking and nervous.

Whoops, thought Vampire Umpire. She hadn't broken up with him the night before?

Molly was unsure what to say. It was a delicate situation and when she searched for the right words to say, her mind went blank. And then, suddenly and numinously, as if a divine voice were speaking them directly into her ear, she said, "True love never has to hide, Ham," she said. "So many people out there they just want to touch you: to kiss up, and rub up and feel up on you."

"Okay...?" he said.

"But I just feel with love, it's like beyond my darkness the person I love will be my light."

Vampire Umpire said, "What if you give him some time to prove that you can trust him?"

"I said be quiet, okay!" Molly yelled. "I believe true love is the greatest weapon," she continued to Ham, "to end the war caused by pain. And that nothing real can be threatened. And I'm sorry, but that's not what I feel for you."

"I understand," he said.

"Plus," she took his hands in both of hers and peered up at him, squinting a little sadly, "you're interrupting my grinding."

"Stop interrupting her grinding," Vampire Umpire added in chorus.

Ham walked out the door, his perfect posture warped into a crook-backed question mark by sadness.

"I don't know where that came from," Molly said, "but that might be the best break up speech I've ever given."

"Are you kidding? Those were literally all lyrics from All Night by Beyoncé. You shamelessly ripped all of them off."

"I did?"

"Oh wait, no. The grinding thing came from an earlier song on the album. Sorry, I think."

"Oh, you don't need to apologise" said Molly.

"No, the *song* is called Sorry."

"Ah. Well as long as he doesn't figure the lyric thing out, I should be fine, right?"

"Definitely. Plus, no offence but he's not that sharp, so I think everything will be okay."

"Goood," she said. "So where are we off to next?"

"Ugh," said Vampire Umpire. "Unfortunately for us, we have a retreat in the woods, to 'promote a spirit of team spirit' according to the schedule."

"A spirit of team spirit?"

"Don't worry: it's a metaphorical spirit. No more ghosts." He zipped shut the last suitcase and placed it in a pile of five beside the door. Molly travelled light, in part because she still refused to use any of her tennis winnings to buy any actual tennis equipment of her own, and all her clothes and necessary items were in a single large backpack. Vampire Umpire preferred to enjoy as many comforts as he could carry, and on top of a large wardrobe also travelled with a decent portable library and a good collection of fine scents and pomades.

"So then what's the problem?"

"Camping?" said Vampire Umpire. "Plus I'm literally surrounded by thousands of deadly stakes all just sticking out of the ground. One fall and I could die for all eternity."

"Yeah, those are called trees," she said. "Don't worry, it's going to be fun!"

◆

"This is no fun," Molly said sourly. "I'm bored and cold and the woods smell."

Molly was sitting just inside their tent, poking her head just outside the slightly open flap, staring out at the trees. It had rained incessantly during the camping expedition and the leaves of the trees were plastered flat and wet like the coiffure of an evil Japanese ghost girl who had had a bucket of water dumped on them by a prospective victim on what had already been a bad hair day. As the bulk of the team-building experiences had been dependant on clement weather, the days and evenings had passed in brief scurries through the showers to the tents of friends to chat, or – and in Molly's case this was more common – in aggressive napping in protest against the entire experience.

The one excitement was the shoe thief, who had been sneaking at night to one tent or another and stealing pairs of shoes. There was an ongoing bet in the campgrounds about who was stealing the shoes, and the pool had reached over two thousand pounds.

The sun, weak as overly diluted orange squash and barely discernible beneath the storm clouds, which were as dark grey and thick as George Clooney's pubic hair, slipped below the horizon. Vampire Umpire stepped out into the night. "Ah, fresh air," he said. "Ewwww."

"I know, right?" Molly said. The air carried a scent like wet dog, but a wet dog that had been eating a whole bunch of rancid meat.

After too many days in a tent in the woods, it no longer surprised Molly to see Vampire Umpire was immaculately dressed in a well cut suit and a shirt pressed so flat it was like it had been ironed with Benedict Cumberbatch's cheekbones. His shoes, despite his regular walks in the woods, were perfectly polished and black as a lake on a still, moonless night.

He held his hand out flat, palm up, in the air for several seconds, then drew it back, entirely dry. "The rain's stopping," he said. "Would you like me to make a fire? It'd warm you a bit, and you could roast marshmallows."

"Ooooh, yes please, Campfire Umpire." Vampire Umpire walked into the woods. The stench grew even stronger, and he was very glad he didn't have to breathe if he chose not. The rain had of course soaked through most of the ground, and he had to hunt hard in the ground near the boles to find dry sticks and twigs. In one, slicked black with mud, he found a single discarded tennis trainer. It had been part shredded, and he added the foam lining to his pile, assuming it would burn fast.

The sky was bleak but empty when he returned to the tent and assembled the fire. Molly warmed her hands over it from within the tent. "Hold on a second," she said. A long skewer, three marshmallows impaled on it so viciously that it reminded Vampire Umpire of an old colleague of his now passed to the other lands, appeared out of the tent and waved haphazardly in the air over the fire. Vampire Umpire graciously and subtly held the end to steady it slightly as the marshmallows toasted.

"So what do you plan to do tonight?" he asked her.

"The shoe pool is way up now," Molly said. "I'm going to watch the tents and see if I can catch the perp."

"Oooh, nice use of the lingo."

"Thanks, I've been watching Veronica Mars again."

"Yes, I know, we've been sharing a tent roughly the size of a Ryan Air toilet cubical."

"Please, you know a Ryan Air toilet cubical is just one of their coffee pots."

"*Exactly.*"

♦

Night fell and one by one the glow of the tents was extinguished from within, like coals cooling. Vampire Umpire stood, posture perfect, in the shadows just outside the campsite. Beside him, Molly crouched wearing a thick winter jacket with a duvet wrapped around her. She was holding night vision binoculars to her eyes and scanning back and forth over the tents.

"Over there," she said, and pointed.

One of the tents was being unzipped and a man was slipping out. He was dressed all in black and was looking around furtively. Vampire Umpire used his vampire powers of concealment to make sure he and Molly remained invisible, even though they were probably far enough away to be invisible anyway.

"Let's follow," Molly whispered. She began to creep forward, hunched over and taking slow long steps on the balls of her feet. Vampire Umpire walked normally beside her, perfectly silent.

"What vampire power is that?" she asked.

"It's just natural grace and poise," Vampire Umpire countered.

The man exited the campground and they followed. He didn't turn and they had no idea who he was from behind, though Molly could feel curiosity gnawing at her the way she might gnaw at a block of delicious cheese. A taxi was waiting for the man and he stepped in and drove off. "Hold on," Vampire Umpire said. He cradled Molly in his arms and ran after the car. It was odd, Molly thought: for some reason though Vampire Umpire's heart didn't beat, it didn't feel cold when he held her.

After perhaps twenty minutes they were in a seedy area of town. The taxi stopped on the other side of a street from a building on which rested a tall neon line drawing of a topless woman. Underneath it was a sign reading "The Sin-agogue: The World's Only Jewish Strip Club." Vampire Umpire and Molly watched as the man walked in; as he did, the sign's light fell on him and they saw Jebediah Moslius' face, slicked down in blue and pink like a teen at a rave.

"God damn it," Molly said. "It's just Moslius being pervy again."

"We should go," said Vampire Umpire.

"Yeah," said Molly, clearly disappointed.

"Of course, first we should call in a report on the fire I am nearly one hundred per cent sure I smell at the Sin-agogue, maybe alerting the press to the exciting incident as it will help stimulate their sales, which is important as a free, lively press is important in an increasingly tense political climate."

"Yeah!" said Molly.

◆

When they got back to the campground, they saw a large shadow looming over one of the tents. Vampire Umpire could hear Molly's muscles tense beside him.

"The shoe thief!" she hissed.

The shadow raced away from the tent. In the dark night there were no details, only the impression of long limbs loping over the ground. Molly raced after it, not making any effort to be quiet, and the thing turned and saw her and sped away even faster. Molly and Vampire Umpire gave chase, charging after the thief into the woods.

There was only the foul stench that had haunted the campground all week and the rustle and crash of their chase through the fallen branches and shed leaves. Vampire Umpire and Molly seemed to be gaining ground, then ceding it, and in the uneven terrain and the low visibility it was impossible to say for sure how their pursuit went.

The world went silent right as they entered a clearing. Both stopped and they looked around, hunting for any trace of their quarry. "Oh my god," Molly said.

"What?"

She pointed upwards. Vampire Umpire followed her finger and saw in the trees above them weird flaps of some strange material hanging from the branches. There were long skinny tendrils like stripped veins and thicker, chunkier lumps. Her hands shaking, Molly turned on the torch on her phone and shone it on the strange sky burial ground.

Hundreds, perhaps thousands, of trainers hung above their heads. They were eviscerated and torn, and no shoe seemed to hang with its partner. In particular, the toe box of each shoe had been busted open as if from within.

Something screamed, low and guttural, and the trees across from them swayed from side to side, battered apart with some tremendous force. Molly turned to face the monster and in her thoughtless motion the light fell on the beast, framing it perfectly.

The creature loomed at least eight feet tall. It was covered all over in chestnut brown hair as thick and luscious as Jon Hamm's but smeared with slightly more mud and excrement. Its arms hung well below its knees and were sinewy and as developed as a steroid abuser's. Its long legs were all muscle too, and ended in a huge pair of red Nike tennis shoes.

It stared at them, poised in the moment between fight and flight like Schrodinger's cat if it had got super pissed about the whole 'being forcibly enclosed in a box of poison' thing. Vampire Umpire stepped forward. He spoke, "Grruuuwwooooruuughhhaaa."

"You speak its language?" Molly asked.

Vampire Umpire coughed. "No, I just swallowed an insect when we ran through the woods. Noble Bigfeet," he continued. "We mean you no harm. Enjoy your treasures and know we will trespass no further."

The creature seemed to breathe more easily, and Vampire Umpire began to back away, gesturing to Molly to do the same. His eyes never left those of the beast until they were out of the clearing, after which he took Molly's hand and lead her quickly out of the forest.

"Why did you call that Bigfoot a Bigfeet?" Molly asked.

"Well that's its proper name," he said. "It has two big feet after all, not just one. Otherwise it would be tripping over all the time."

"So it was stealing the shoes all along."

"Yes," said Vampire Umpire. "Grabbing trainer after comfortable trainer but always finding them too small. And so, in their rage, the Bigfeets tear the shoes apart and cast them at the sky, to try to strike down the God that taunts them with comfortable footwear in impossibly tiny sizes."

"I had no clue they were real," Molly said.

"They're very real. And quite common. Many of them only want socks, to keep their bare feet warm when winter arrives.

So have you ever noticed your socks disappearing from your laundry?"

"You mean...?"

"Nah, usually they're just getting caught in a filter, or it's a simple pairing problem where one of the socks gets washed and the other in a pair doesn't, creating the illusion that one is lost."

"Oh."

"But about half the time, it's a local Bigfeet, stealing the footwear it loves so much but is usually to well-foot-endowed to wear. They're all foot fetishists, you know."

"It is a strange and beautiful world," said Molly.

"Filled with sights wonderful and terrible," Vampire Umpire said.

Molly nodded, "Like when you go to the gym, and sneak into the men's side, and there's a really hot guy in the shower but also a really not hot guy."

Chapter Nine

One month and four tennis tournaments passed, alarmingly quickly, the tempus fugiting as if in a single sentence in an excellent novel. They had arrived in Rome, and Vampire Umpire and Molly were renting a suite of rooms in a palazzo on the outskirts of the city. To be more accurate, Vampire Umpire was renting it; Molly was living in one of the rooms.

The walls of the palazzo were coated thickly in classic romantic frescos, and in between the gold filigreed pilasters were well-sculpted caryatids and telamons. The walls curved in graceful arcs to domed ceilings, each of which was also garnished with paintings, largely of notable Italian political figures from the middle ages, not one of whom either could identify. It was important, Vampire Umpire thought, to remember how transitory political moments were, even during the most turbulent times. Human progress eventually always… trumps idiotic leadership that may seem, by conservative estimates, too cruel not to do irreversible harm

While the floors were marble, they were covered in thick Persian rugs and held the warmth of the sun so strongly that the pair kept the windows open constantly. Their rooms were high enough above the street that the scents and sounds of the traffic were diffused to a tolerable level. The distance reduced the often harsh street conversations to a pleasant musical burble of vowel sounds.

Vampire Umpire leafed through the mail. "We got our passes for the tennis club," he said, sorting out both his and Molly's and placing them on a rococo table with legs so thin they were like Kate Moss's if she were double anorexic. The legs were carved so excessively that Molly expected the table to collapse should a mosquito fly rapidly above it, but so far it had held up to the weight of Vampire Umpire's keys and now the plastic photo ID cards. "And there is a parcel for you."

"I'll open it later," she said. They each had plans in the city. Vampire Umpire locked the door behind them and they started walking down the stairs.

"Do you feel like dinner tonight?" Vampire Umpire asked. "I'll cook."

Vampire Umpire had no nutritional investment in food, but he enjoyed cooking and he enjoyed the scents and the flavours. And after several centuries of practice, even the least sedulous person's cooking skills would be fairly like a hunting dog spotting a rabbit – on point. "Sounds good to me," Molly said.

She stepped out into the dazzling sunlight and pulled on a pair of sunglasses. "I'll see you later?" she asked.

"Sure," said Vampire Umpire. He walked down into the palazzo's basement and opened the secret door that lead into the catacombs.

♦

Tyrone Ennis was waiting in a limo at the end of the street. "Thank you so much for agreeing to do this," he said to her.

"Not a problem," she said. "You did say we would get ice cream after though, right?"

"I don't remember discussing that, but I'm sure we can find a gelateria if you like."

"You paying?"

"Of course it will be my treat."

"YES!" said Molly, and then began singing a song of her own creation that primarily featured the lyrics, "I'mma eat gelato, Mr Roberto" repeated as ad nauseam as she would probably be after all the ice cream she planned to eat. It was arguably racially insensitive, but charming enough in her delivery and in her innocent glee that she easily got away with it.

The car was easing through the traffic like a laxative-aided bowel movement. Tyrone Ennis let Molly continue singing for perhaps ten to fifteen minutes before trying to regain her attention. "So it is very important to observe protocol through the entire meeting," he said. "The cardinal will run through everything with you, but just remember you're representing the entire tennis community."

"That's cool," Molly said. "I wasn't planning to swear or anything. And I'll only hit him if he swings at me first." Her eyes narrowed at the thought, and unconsciously she pounded her right fist hard into her left palm. It made a sound like an unstoppable force meeting an immovable object.

"Ms. Durand, I find it very unlikely that the Pope is going to 'take a swing' at you, to use your redolent phrase."

"He'd better not, if he likes solid food," she said. "Though I guess maybe he just has gelato all the time?"

◆

Vampire Umpire walked through the Roman catacombs, sidestepping the occasional rat. He consulted no map, having spent too many years underground here in his early years as a vampire. He deftly transcribed the narrow labyrinthine tangle of passages that separated the catacombs of San Valentino and the wider, more ornate tunnels below San Sebastiano. He was soon above ground again, climbing the stairs in the basilica.

He waited in the shadows of entrance for perhaps five minutes before Ioana arrived. "I am really excited to see the sights," she said.

"It is not a problem. Rome is filled with art, and with no guide it can be hard to make sense of it. Like staring at the stars with no knowledge of the constellations, one can be overwhelmed by the light."

He lead her into the first cubiculum, with Bernini's sculpture of Saint Sebastian and then on through the series of demons painted in triptych by Cerasa. She listened enthralled as he told her the stories behind the images, and occasionally took his hand to drag him back, so she could stare at some particular painting for a time far longer than he had initially allotted. Her eyes blazed with hunger.

They spent the entire afternoon within the basilica. When they were done, he walked her back to the entrance. The sun had not yet set; he could not walk her home, so he made an excuse that he had left something in the building. What would a human want so much that it could excuse such rudeness? he wondered. Then, it came to him. "I have to leave you here, Ioana," he said. "I've lost my anti-diarrhoea pills somewhere on our tour, and must urgently go look for them." Perfect, he thought: his answer was both suave and showed a reluctance to soil himself that would cause anyone to admire his commitment to hygiene.

'Thank you for taking me," she said. She held his arm, just below the bicep, for a moment, then let her hand fall and turned away.

"Would you like to join Molly and I for dinner tonight?" he asked.

"No thanks," Ioana replied quickly. "I have plans. With Jeb." She walked into the light and down the street rapidly. Vampire Umpire watched until she disappeared from view and then headed back into the boneyard, which is what a catacomb effectively is but would also be a great name for an all male brothel.

He sat quietly among his fellow dead, thinking of his burgeoning friendship with Ioana and his dear friend Molly, and wondering how, having spent centuries longing to be a tennis umpire, his dream had come true so easily and so satisfyingly. He had lived a long life, and in any life happiness and misery weigh about equally in the balance. But lately he had known joys beyond any he had expected.

◆

"Is it true I am meant to call the pope Papa Burgundy?" Molly asked the cardinal. "Y'know, because of the red robes?"

"Cardinals wear the red," the Cardinal said. His name was Lieurich, but there was little need to remember it as he was unlikely to be a recurring character. "Though some do refer to the Pope as Il Papa, the father."

"Gotcha," said Molly. "I'll call him Big Daddy."

"Please do not," Tyrone Ennis said.

"The pope loves tennis," the cardinal said, "and he has apparently enjoyed watching your matches particularly this year. So he wishes to simply greet you, offer you a blessing for your performance in the Rome tournament, and have perhaps a few moments of conversation with you. Rulers and nobility petition for months for a mere nod of acknowledgement, so you are highly honoured."

"Jeez, fine. I'll give him my hardest high five."

"Just bend over his hand when he offers it. Mr. Ennis, you may wait here if you wish."

Tyrone Ennis stood alone in the antechamber outside the Holy Office, looking small and worried as Molly and the cardinal walked towards and through the large wooden door that seemed heavy enough that it probably offered the Pope as much protection as the two armed guards who flanked it. He wrung his hands together, like a man drying a dish towel, and in fact nervousness had brought enough sweat to his palms that some few drips of water did splash on the floor.

Molly walked into the office. The man sitting at the desk rose, and walked towards her, holding his hands in front of him like a dog that had just learned to beg and wants more delicious treats. "Watching your matches," the man said, "I sense brief moments of the divine brought to flesh as God never has before. To see you play is to see the finest, noblest possibilities of the human race made manifest and tangible."

"Sorry, who are you?" she said.

"I am Pope Francis," he said.

"Uhhh, what?" Molly turned to the cardinal. "What happened to the good pope? You know, John Paul Ringo the Third or whatever? The nice one."

The cardinal froze. "We have had two popes since St. John Paul the Great," he finally managed to utter.

"Ohhhhh, yeah. There was that weird Nazi pope," Molly said.

"We try not to mention him," the cardinal said hastily.

"Listen, sorry dude, but I only really wanted to meet the good pope. I'm outtie five thousand." She walked out the door, casually pulling out her phone to check her messages.

"Outtie five thousand," Pope Francis said thoughtfully. "That *would* be a fresh closing line for my next sermon."

♦

"So we both had good days," Molly said as she sopped the last few drops of meat and sauce of her plate with the garlic bread Vampire Umpire had ever so carefully hand baked for her. "I got three different scoops of ice cream, each more delicious than the last, and Tyrone Ennis paid for them all."

"Nice! And your meeting with the Pope?"

"What? Oh, right. I think that was cancelled."

"So what are your plans for the rest of the evening?"

"I dunno. I've got six trophies now, plus the plaque for winning the rap battle. I was figuring I'd throw them in a big heap on my bedroom floor and make a Smaug pile, then just roll around on them for a while."

"That does sound fun," Vampire Umpire said. "I think I might go out sight seeing." He walked towards the door. "Oh," he said. "Your parcel."

"Cool!" said Molly. "I hope it's sweets!" It was sitting on the table still. She unwrapped the brown paper in which it was swaddled. Inside was a plain rosewood box, with a small metal bolt locking it. She slid the bold out, then opened the lid. Vampire Umpire heard a click and with all his vampire speed he charged at Molly, throwing her towards the sofa, using his vampire strength and his vampire precision, and shielding her with his body.

A tendril of something somewhere between a shadow and a curlicue of smoke coiled out from the box. It quested in the air for a moment, like a snake scenting prey, and then stabbed forward. Vampire Umpire grabbed for it, but it slipped through his fingers like water and plunged deep into his chest.

"Are you okay?" Molly asked. She was walking towards him. His thoughts felt slow and every moment was a struggle against titanic forces.

"Stay back," he said. "It might not be safe."

He fell, knocking the table over and sending the box flying into the far corner of the room. It rolled a few times, and the lid cracked and shattered completely between the second and third rotation. Molly could see it was now entirely empty.

She walked over to Vampire Umpire. He didn't respond to any of her calls, or her light finger taps on his cheeks and chest. She could do nothing but watch as his pallor turned from the white of marble to a sickly grey.

Chapter Ten

It had taken all of her strength, but Molly had finally managed to move Vampire Umpire into his bed. She had no clue how to treat him – did vampires feel the cold, or need warmth? Should she make chicken soup, or like blood soup? But wasn't blood soup just like a kind of warm black pudding? He remained as grey and bleak as the skies in Aberdeen had been.

She watched him through the night, but there was no change. She would have traded terrifying amounts of money or cataclysmic losses to have spoken to him for even a minute. Both just to hear his voice and to ask what the correct medical treatment for vampires was. And maybe also got his recipe for garlic bread – she could still taste it and it went down smooth, like a well-oiled gigolo.

Finally, she decided to check his wallet. He kept an old fashioned one, more like a document case, in which he stored a variety of necessities, from money to legal contracts to his calendar. She smiled thinking of it. Actually, to him it probably still counted as ahead of the times. Perhaps in another couple of hundred years he would have a money clip. She wondered if he would live through the night, and felt the smile wither on her face like grapes on the vine in winter.

She searched through the assortment of papers. Plenty of money; she idly placed a few million lire in her pocket, almost without realising it. She found a book filled with a list of addresses and phone numbers in Vampire Umpire's elegant copperplate writing, but all of the information was for businesses or contractors. She dumped the book on the floor in despair and a small shim of paper slid out. She picked it up.

It was a thick piece of white card. There was a border embossed around it, but no ink on the embossing so she could only discern it by running her fingers over it. She turned the card and on the other side was a mobile phone number and no other information whatsoever.

She dialled the number. It was answered after four long rings. "Yeah?" spoke a male voice of indeterminate accent.

"Hi," she said. "Ummm…" Molly had no clue what to say, where to begin explaining her situation or even if she should, given she had no idea to whom she was speaking.

"How did you get this number?" the man asked. She still hesitated. "I'm about three seconds from hanging up," the man said. "If this is Kevin Spacey again, I told you: I'm not interested, and I can hear you breathing. Just take no for an answer, and if you have to masturbate to my voice, you can buy one of my audiobooks, like your mum did."

"I found you card," she said finally. "In my friend's stuff."

"Who's your friend?"

"His name is Vampire Umpire," she said.

"Shit. Is he okay?"

Molly explained the situation finally. "Where are you?" the man said. "I'll be there as fast as I can." She told him.

"Should I…" she said. "Y'know, give him blood or something?"

"Don't do anything," the man said. "And blood is the last thing he needs right now. I'll be at the airport in an hour. Pick me up."

"How can you get here so fast?"

"That's my business."

"How will I know you?"

"It's simple: I'll be the handsomest person there, won't I?"

♦

At the airport, Molly looked around the crowds cautiously. Finally, she saw a man with hair as black as a dead iPhone and a face that would have made a sculptor go "dang that's a *really* nice face," because sculptors aren't poets and are not necessarily good with words. So, you ask, why wouldn't said praise-filled hypothetical sculptor carve the lovely face they beheld? Well, screw you buddy: they don't just sculpt stuff when they see it because marble is really, really expensive. You have a hell of an attitude. The man was wearing an obviously tailored suit that almost caressed the smooth musculature of his frame.

Molly walked up to him, pushing her way through the crowds of loud reunions and parting lovers in tear-stained embraces and the grand parade of families feuding at the beginning of their holiday. "You must be Vampire Umpire's friend," she said.

"Mi dispiace, io non parlo inglese e tu mi stanno spaventando," the man said. His voice was as rich and lovely as the world's sexiest billionaire and, like a lower spinal column injury, it made her weak at the knees.

"I think you want me," the strange voice she recognised from the phone said, and she turned. The man had messy brown hair roughly the colour of a sodden sewer rat's, and a face that could probably be called a face if she were being charitable. He was wearing a long black coat, crumpled and stained in several places, and a too-large shirt in which silver cufflinks sparkled like diamonds in a slag pile. He wore a pair of suit trousers, under which a large pair of boots completed his ensemble. "Molly, right?"

"Yes," she said. "You're not quite what I expected."

"Well that's why expectations are a bad thing. They make an expec out of tat and ions. You bring a car?"

"A taxi," she said.

"Nice to meet you, by the way," the man said, shaking her hand. His fingers were long but strong and his palms soft as expensive toilet paper. "I'm Dr. Ross Macpherson." He paused. She made no sign of recognition. He shrugged. "Okay, take me there."

♦

In the taxi, Molly turned towards the odd man and said, "How did you get here? You didn't have enough time for you to get through airport security, let alone fly from anywhere."

Ross waved his hand across the air. His fingers almost seemed to glow, which Molly ascribed to a trick of the moonlight glimmering over his fingers, which judging by his portly figure she bet were pretty greasy from constant snacking. "You've not known Vampire Umpire long, have you?"

"About 2 months," she said.

"So you should know now the world is a stranger place than most people think," he said. He made a contemptuous gesture at the crowds of pedestrians thronging the pavements. "Most of you people don't know that, because of people like me."

"So what are you?" she said, a hint of disgust in her voice. She didn't like the arrogant, unpleasant man, and she felt certain he could never help her friend. "Some kind of policeman?"

"Fuck no," he said. "I'm a doctor."

"But of what?"

"Originally of science," he said. "But now you might say that just as a medical doctor handles ailments of the body, I deal with more… spiritual concerns."

Molly saw they were approaching the palazzo and she said to the driver, "Here please." The driver responded in no way, not even acknowledging he'd heard her. "Hey, excuse me!" she said again.

"Oh, he can't hear you," Ross said. "Hold on." He waved his hand in the air and again there was that eerie glimmer. "Stop here, mate," he said to the driver. The driver immediately pulled the car over.

"Okay, what was that?" Molly asked.

"A simple spell," he said. "I felt we needed privacy."

◆

In the room, Dr. Macpherson bent over Vampire Umpire's chest and listened for a while. "Close the curtains," he said. While Molly obeyed, he stripped off the bedcovers and ripped open Vampire Umpire's tuxedo and shirt, baring his torso. He reached into his bag and withdrew a vial of some thick orange fluid and began to paint runic looking sigils on the vampire's naked skin and on the sheets surrounding him. He worked quickly but for a long time, and soon the vampire was enclosed in a circle of symbols as meaningless to Molly as writing was to most of the modern citizens of the world.

Dr. Macpherson knelt beside the bed. He took a knife from his bag and scored his palm, then clenched his palms together. The blood oozed between his fingers, and he sprinkled a few droplets into the circle, careful that none landed on Vampire Umpire. He began to chant, strange words with too many consonants and unnatural rhythms.

Molly watched, and from all across Vampire Umpire's chest beads of black smoke began to seep out, as if he were sweating crude oil, by which I mean unprocessed oil, not oil that just swears a lot or says bad innuendoes. The smoke began to gather above his chest, forming once again into the serpent-like form that had attacked them. Dr. Macpherson stared at it. Earlier he had placed a vessel on the floor, an ancient urn carved in silver, and he began to gesture at the smoke creature, as if drawing it towards the vessel.

It didn't respond at all. It lashed once at the air and suddenly fire sprang up in exactly the places where the paint lay on the sheets. Dr. Macpherson stared at it questioningly for only a moment before ceasing his chant, and the beast sank back into Vampire Umpire's flesh. Macpherson spoke a few words, in character so different to his original chant that Molly sensed it must be another language, and the flames died out like discmen in the iPod's world.

"Whoever sent that truly longed for his death," Dr. Macpherson said.

"It was for me," she said. "The parcel anyway."

"Do you have it still?" She collected everything for him: the box, the torn paper, the broken lid. He placed everything on the floor and knelt over the pile. He looked at everything, sniffed the packaging, even tasted the box with his tongue.

"No trace of the sender," he said. "Even the address label is typed." He waved his hand over the material, intoning another spell. A green orb formed in the air, then fizzled. "Not even any magical traces," he said. "That was a tracking spell that should have followed the trail back to whoever placed this curse."

"Curse?"

He stood, knocking dust of his knees. "It's a death curse," he said. "I suppose intended for you, but a curse isn't particularly targeted: it feels only the intensity of its creator's hate."

"Is he going to die?" Molly asked. She remembered all the moments with Vampire Umpire, the sound of his voice and the scent of his body next to her, and she thought that the world had seemed so much brighter during the short time he had known him, and would be a far emptier place if he were absent from it.

Dr. Ross Macpherson thought. "I have held the thing back, so it will do no more harm, but I can't withdraw it," he said, "and if I cannot there is no magician on earth who can." He spoke plainly, as if stating a fact instead of boasting.

"So there's nothing we can do?" She felt tears pricking her eyes like slipped false eyelashes.

His brow furrowed deeply, though it was hard to tell as his face was marred with more wrinkles than a Shar pei's scrotum, and his eyes darkened, as if he were considering some terrible thought. "There might be one thing," he said. "But it will be difficult, and you will need to trust me."

"Okay," she said. "Anything."

"And we're going to need an in with the Vatican."

"Ahhh," she said. "Now that might be a problem."

◆

Tyrone Ennis had not been pleased when she woke him, but when he heard another of his employees had been attacked he acted promptly. He dictated the cardinal's address to her, and told her if she needed anything else, just to call.

The cardinal was less readily responsive. Lieurich held the door against them. He was dressed in a night-robe, which, under other circumstances, might have struck Molly as adorable.

"Ms. Durand, no-one has ever treated the pope with such rudeness and lack of consideration, and I am the one who brought you before him. If you think I will make that mistake twice you are as foolish as you are discourteous."

"Ouch," said Dr. Macpherson. "Want to go check yourself into the sick burns ward, Molly?"

The cardinal slammed the door on them, or would have, if Ross' boot had not been blocking it. Experimentally, he slammed the door once or twice, while Ross watched him impassive, then finally raised an eyebrow. "It's why I wear Doc Martens, innit?" he said. "Block a door faster than a scotch child blocks a toilet."

"I am never going to help you," the cardinal said.

Dr. Macpherson loomed taller suddenly, and his coat seemed to surround him in an aegis made of power and mystery. "I have long walked the secret pathways of this world. I have seen the terrible deeds that men wish others will never learn and the read unacknowledged thoughts they hope remain obscure." He glared down at the cardinal, "You sicken me, but help me and I will keep silent."

The cardinal slumped. "I will help you," he said.

"Cool," said Ross. "Off you pop then and put on some clothes. We want to see him tonight."

Once the cardinal was gone, Molly asked, with sordid curiosity "What was it he did?"

"Oh, no clue. But everyone has some secret they don't want getting out. He probably sneaks extra communion wafers when no-one's looking. Tries to get the nuns drunk and horny on the ol' blood of Christ." He scratched his head. "I always felt that would be a good name for a brand of red wine."

◆

Once again, Molly found herself being lead before the Pope. This time though her previous absolute lack of interest had been replaced with a tense nervousness. The doors opened again and again, the small man at the desk rose to meet her.

"Ms. Durand," he said. "My cardinal tells me I urgently need to see you, but not why."

"I…" Molly realised she had no idea what to say. Unfortunately, Dr. Macpherson stepped forward boldly.

"I need your fragment of the true cross," he said. "And the real one, not some shitty fake, or I'll know."

"Why are you so bad at dealing with people?" Molly asked him. "You can't just demand stuff and people will just do it for you." It was a true sentiment, she reflected. Like, you couldn't just demand someone write you a novel and they would just do it. "It's like you just stride into places and expect everyone to obey you, what, just 'cos you think you're clever?"

Dr. Macpherson she could see was preparing for some speech or trick and she feared the result, when the Pope spoke, forestalling him. "I will grant your request," the Pope said, "if Ms. Durand does one of mine."

"Nothing kinky, Fran," said Ross. "You better keep it fairly clean."

"I will give you the fragment," the Pope said. "But tomorrow Molly has to win her tennis match."

"That should be okay," she said. "I've not lost one yet, even though I still don't actually know the rules of tennis."

"There is a complication," said the Pope.

"Oh?"

"Well," he said. "I have something of a fondness for gambling but I have not been picking many winners lately."

"Yeah, that cardinal you employ's a testament to that," Ross sneered.

The pope smiled. "I hate that guy too. He keeps trying to get my nuns drunk on sacramental wine. But anyway, the result is I have lost the entire Vatican's winter heating budget. So, the only bet I can make with long enough odds to recover it is…"

"What?" asked Molly.

"You have to win tomorrow's match… with only one swing of your racquet," said the Pope.

Molly's mouth opened. "Does it have to be *my* racquet?" she asked. "Because I usually just borrow one."

Chapter Eleven

Dr. Macpherson had offered her spells and curses, had said he would sit in the crowd and use his magic to ensure all the opponent's shots drifted wide of target. Molly had refused though. "It'll be fine," she told him. "For some reason I am really good at tennis."

"But…"

"It will be fine," she said again. She had a sense of him now. He was an arrogant man, unpleasant man who had grown used to being the smartest in the room no matter if that assessment were delusional. As a result he just assumed he had the tribute and respect of everyone in it, and Molly realised that this would sadly forever deny him both. Things always had to be done his way. On a tennis court, though, she was, it seemed, the one without equal.

Her opponent won the coin toss and decided to serve to her. He tossed the ball high in the air and his back snapped liquid and fast as an eel swimming, propelling the ball to her at tremendous speed. Her timing was flawless however, and she swung fast and hard through the ball sending it crashing back over the net to bounce in the court and mash heavily into the man's testicles.

He collapsed on the court groaning and occasionally vomiting. The umpire wandered over to him and lightly prodded him with a questioning toe. After a moment, the umpire said, "Game, set and match, Ms. Durand."

"Not how I expected you to win," Ross said. "But pretty *crushingly* effective."

"Oh, he'll be fine," Molly said. "He'll be healed in a couple of weeks."

"I guess other men might tolerate a couple of weeks of ball pain better than me," Ross said. "Which is probably why all my relationships are so short."

"Plus your face, your character and so many other reasons," she told him. "Like, literally I could fill a book with reasons to hate you. But my friend is in trouble, so instead, let's go see the pope."

◆

They stood over Vampire Umpire again. "Give me your hand," Ross said. Molly held out her right. "Probably the other hand is better," he said. She complied and he slashed his silver knife across her palm.

"You dick," Molly said. "What the fuck?"

"Just take his hand," Ross said, obviously not caring.

Molly held Vampire Umpire's hand. Ross held the fragment of the true cross above his head and began intoning words. She felt her skin ripple with some force and the room and the people in it and even time took on an oneiric texture. Slowly, but as if with inexorable force, like the movement of a tectonic plate, Dr. Macpherson brought the cross down and touched it first to Molly's temple and then to her chest over her heart, following which he did the same to Vampire Umpire. Molly felt a swelling in her veins, and then a sense of tightness, as if a coil of rope had enwrapped her whole.

Dr. Macpherson looked at her. "This is your last chance, Molly. You can turn back now, though he will die. Or you can follow me and we might save him."

"Whatever it takes, I'll do it," she said. "But, actually, I'm not doing any heavy lifting."

"You're already bringing everything we need." He scrawled a pentacle on the floor with chalk. He took a vial of some kind of blood from his bag and uncorked it. "Virgin blood," he said. "Hard to find these days."

"Couldn't you just use your own?"

"Hah. Good one, which I bet no-one's ever said to you after sex." He rolled up his sleeves, and she saw his arms were encrusted with tattoos, each depicting some archaic symbol or some alchemical rune. "Whatever I tell you," he said, while he waved his arms slowly over the pentagram, "you do it immediately."

"Where are we going?" she asked. She could feel fear beginning to grow behind her skull. And, while she had found his number in Vampire Umpire's bag, she didn't at all like this Dr. Macpherson, and despite her promise she found it impossible to entirely trust him.

"Where so many of my former friends and enemies have told me I should go," he said, punctuating the end of his sentence with a tortured gesture of his arms that echoed a deranged mime cracking open a human rib cage. A ragged red wound appeared in the air, dripping pustules of black ichor and red ooze that boiled in the atmosphere and evaporated before striking the ground. Heat blasted from it in waves, like an open furnace. "Hell," he said.

"You timed that deliberately!"

"Can I help it if I'm a natural showman?" he asked, smirking.

"You are *such* a dick," she said.

"Then chase after me," he said. "Like I'm a bone and you're the dog." He paused. "Actually, it is dangerous to go into Hell without taking proper care. I'd better prepare." He sat down on the bed and tied his left bootlace tightly. "There we go." He stood and strode through the portal. Cautiously, almost unconsciously ducking as she neared the threshold, Molly followed.

◆

Hell was less hot than she had imagined, and than aphorisms had suggested. In fact, a snowball might very well have lasted for some time. The ground around their feet seemed coated in a thick, cloying snow. Molly bent to touch it, and Dr. Macpherson stopped her. "I don't think you want to touch that," he said.

"Why not? It ain't yellow."

"Yeah, but it's also not snow." He gestured forwards and she saw a huge smokestack belching out thick, almost clotted clouds of the stuff accompanied by roiling black fumes. The cloudy material mushroomed out and collapsed downwards with each gout, and fell to earth rolling out and down over the smokestack's sides. "It's rendered human fat," he said.

"I'm definitely throwing these shoes out," Molly said. "When we get back."

"If," he said.

He sighed and seemed to gather himself, then started walking. "It's like I'm Virgil and you're Dante," he said. "And you will follow in my wake as I guide you round this place."

"Dante?" she asked.

"He was a poet," Ross said. "He wrote some of the greatest love poems of all time, other than me own and Shakespeare's, and when the object of his love died, he wrote a grand poem that was a tour of the Hell where he feared to find her, and the rest of the afterlife, where he eventually did."

"Will it guide us, here?"

"Fuck no, it was all wrong, wann't?" said Ross. "He never had to visit here. Look at it," he said. "Look around and tell me what writer could capture this?"

Molly finally found herself forced to confront the environment she now dwelled within. Beyond the smokestack towards which they walked was a city, its walls hundreds of feet tall and larded with spikes and cruel barbed hooks all across its breadth and height. Naked people, their flesh rent and ragged in the climb, hung from some hooks, and though others were bare the walls were soaked bright red with never clotting blood. In the machicolations of the parapet stood poles on which human heads were impaled, and though still distant she could hear their agonised cries – they still lived.

"Here is pain and suffering with never any release," said the doctor. "It's like dating a posh girl from Edinburgh."

The city beyond the wall was strewn with spires that reared upwards like broken teeth in a severed jaw. Ragged wings, like oversized bats' wings frayed with age, carried indistinct figures across between the buildings. The constructions themselves were simply wrong, geometrically: a square wall had sides of various lengths but somehow warped space to be simultaneously complete; a window that seemed circular on first glance would with continued inspection seem to spiral in like a tear in the fabric of space. The sight of it seemed to restructure her thoughts, to erode her beliefs of how reality should behave and she felt overwhelmed and lost. Molly looked up, to seek solace in the sight of the the sky, and saw instead above her was a river of thick black fluid wending through a field of rotting wheat. She was thousands of feet above it, like a skydiver plunging towards the ground, and she found vertigo overwhelming her. She clutched at Dr. Macpherson's arm until she finally accepted she wasn't falling. She released his arm, feeling sheepish for her fear and disgusted at taking comfort from this man and the feel of his soft, squishy ectomorphic arm. Cautiously she looked up again. Small figures moved in the wheat, lifting the dead crops and devouring them avidly.

"Hell doesn't actually lie at the centre of the Earth," he said. "But it wraps around as if it did — as a physicist I would say it occupies some kind of different Hilbertian space aligned contrary to our own, but who really knows how the powers here work? Magic and physics are fundamentally both equally gibberish at this level."

They continued on to the city. The air was riddled with the sound of nictitating insects. They walked past pits of the same black fluid as the river, which sent gusts of acrid scent towards them that made Molly cough to the point of retching. One was close to the road, and she saw a skinless figure within stare at her with eyes devoid of all hope. It slipped beneath the surface, then kicking and splashing reared up again, and she saw its hands grasp futilely at the slick glass slides of the pit. The muscle fibres in its arms began to blister and peel.

"Dante said abandon all hope before you enter, about Hell," said Ross. "Maybe this is removing the last of their hope before they are allowed into the city? But who can say." He gestured his hands and spoke a spell and the person in the pit died. Molly felt grateful that at least they no longer suffered, but a moment later the body writhed again with life. "All these people," Ross continued, his voice affectless, "and we can help none of them."

The road now was lined with trees and on each tree hung a crucified person adorned with a crown of molten steel that seared against their skin and bared their skulls. Skeletal ravens lined the branches and occasionally swept down on bone wings to worry at the flesh of the tormented. The trees oozed a dark crimson sap.

"This will do," Ross said. "Follow me." He walked over towards one of the trees. "Stand under it," he said, indicating a branch where the flow was heavier and more rapid than most, like that of the rapper Nas compared to any of his contemporaries.

"Are you joking?"

"Just do it, as Nike say."

"But my outfit…?"

"What did it cost? Fifty quid?"

Molly was quiet. Actually in total, including socks and shoes, it had cost her fifteen pounds, but that was still a lot of money.

"Yes," she said. "Fifty quid." Her voice cracked slightly on the lie.

"I'll pay you when we get back," he said, and pushed her under the fall. She stood, letting the sap run over her. It stung her flesh slightly, like a dilute acid or groping a sweaty man when your hands are cut. He made her wait under it until she felt as if the sap had soaked into her skin and now infected to the very core of her being.

They walked back to the path and as they stepped onto it she saw a patch where the ground was clear and below was the road, bare to her eyes for the first time. It was composed entirely of jawless skulls, still partially clad with skin. The skulls were arrayed face up, and the eyes stared at the sky and occasionally blinked. She felt the urge to vomit, but Dr. Macpherson already was some distance ahead and she didn't want to be lost here – she was unsure if he would even try to find her. Reluctantly she stepped onto the road and chased after him.

The gates of Hell reared at least fifty feet tall and were fashioned of solid, carved pieces of a single bone. She wished never to meet the creature from which they had come. The gates were illustrated with scrimshaw of people undergoing all manner of torments, and she did not dare stare at it too long. Surprisingly, there were no guards, but then she considered that in practice probably few people tried to break into Hell.

Ross strode through the gates and walked down one of the avenues and she followed. The paving stones continued their cruel and hideous nature. She could see the buildings in detail now, and even the smallest dwelling dwarfed them. Some were made of stone without join, as if some gargantuan slab had been placed and carved and hollowed to make the building in one piece. Others were made of bone, crushed into powder and formed into bricks with blood as the binding clay. These bricks were held together with wrappings of sinew and ligament.

"Why are there no people?" she asked.

"The humans are inside," he said. "Sometimes they get moved between the torture mills but that happens once every century and only I have ever seen it. The demons, well…" He stepped quickly towards her and traced the shape of an eye on her forehead.

Suddenly the streets bustled with life unlike any she had ever seen. Hideous beasts thronged the avenues, and her mind revolted at the sight of them. "It's worse than visiting Swansea at night," she moaned in horror.

Some of the demons were taller than the buildings it seemed, etiolated creatures of ash with limbs thin as thread. Their bodies were dotted with strange red apertures that oscillated seemingly at random as she passed, until she realised they were following her motion. Eyeless creatures of boiled-pink flesh floated in the air. One of them opened its mouth and she saw row upon row of stiletto-sharp teeth. A throbbing gristle creature wandered, organs hanging around its body like stylish accoutrements. She watched as its hearts beat in sequence, saw the roiling pulsations of its stomach sac as it digested food. Was it worse than the 2016 Chanel Spring-Summer line? No, and probably it was cheaper, but still – not good. And all of them had that strange wrongness that made the buildings so intolerable to her sight. It was too much.

"Enough!" she shouted, clawing at the mark Dr. Macpherson had traced on her forehead to no avail. He grabbed her hands and pushed them aside, and ran one cool palm over her brow.

"I'm sorry," he said. "I forgot what it's like the first time you see them."

The street was empty again. But as they walked, she noticed the doctor occasionally swayed aside or took some deviation as if around a person or a crowd, and she realised he saw these things all the time.

They arrived at a palace of carved marble and gold. It had the cold fascistic echoes of brutalist architecture, but refined to a platonic perfection that no human architect had ever equalled. They walked through corridors lined with artworks as hideous and terrible as they were perfectly executed, and floored with carpets of silk as red and flowing as fresh-spilled blood.

The stench of Hell was like that of a putrefying wound, but here the air became somewhat more clear. The scent of roses, Molly realised, was what now flavoured the air, and though at first it was a relief it soon became so overpowering that she longed to breathe again even the smog-clogged air of Rome. But she remembered her friend Vampire Umpire lying near death and suddenly it was easy to gather her resolve.

They entered a throne room lined liberally with the aforescented roses, and carpeted in their shed blossoms. Pillars reared high towards a ceiling beyond Molly's sight. Tiered stairs curved up, like the sweep of a violin's sides, towards a dais of ivory three dozen feet high. On it sat a man who was somehow exquisitely beautiful, even though his hair was blond.

His skin was alabaster and his lips a ruby slash in his flesh with a vaguely lubricious set. His eyes were as green as stolen emeralds, and beholding them engendered the same sense of guilt. His cheekbones were fine and well shaped as exquisitely cast porcelain. His body was slender, but though at repose there was the sense of tremendous power waiting to be unleashed, like a lion sleeping, or a really powerful toaster with some kind of huge fuck off fuse in its plug. Like maybe 4800 W even.

He stared down at them, and Molly sensed that even had their positions been reversed, he would still have managed this feat. "Dr. Macpherson," he said, and his baritone voice rang as clear and true as a singer's about the room. "To what do I owe the honour of a visit from the Master of the Mystic Arts?" This title, which Molly had never heard apportioned to Ross before, was spoken with absolute contumely.

Dr. Macpherson stood at the bottom of the stairs and stared up. He rubbed a hand slowly over the patchy stubble grizzling his jaw. "What up, Lucifer?" he said. "I've got a deal for you, if you want it."

Chapter Twelve

Lucifer stared down at Dr. Macpherson for a moment and a blush glowed in his cheeks like a dying star burning out in one last flaring red supernova. He laughed coldly, and Molly sensed he was furious. "You dare to bargain again with me?" Lucifer asked, his teeth, so white they were almost crystalline, bared like a wolf's. "When all of Hell chatters of how falsely you played me before?"

"I just proposed the deal," Ross said. "You agreed to it." He turned to Molly. "It's like playing monopoly – if someone accepts a trade that's bad for them, is it my fault? Is it really like I, I dunno, *outsmarted* them?" He gazed up at the figure on the dais and cocked one eyebrow. Even Molly found herself wanting to hit him.

One moment Lucifer sat in his throne, the next he stood before them and his hand was around Dr. Ross Macpherson's throat, lifting him high in the air. "Con man," the King of Hell intoned, "let us see you work your tricks without your breath." Up close, he smelled of scorched flesh. "Have you any last requests?" he asked of Ross, "before I crush your throat and chain your companion in my dungeons for ten thousand years of torment unfathomable to mortal minds?"

"You're... going... to... make... her... listen... to... Coldplay?" Ross asked in words choked out and sibilant. Lucifer threw him across the hall, where his body crashed against the wall and onto the ground, sending up a spray of rose petals. Dr. Macpherson stood up and strained at some pain real or imagined in his neck. "Gotta say, Lucy. You make me wish I had time to go to the gym."

"It would take a stupider being than I not to see that this arrogance must come from some extraordinary belief that what you have to offer, I cannot refuse," Lucifer said. "And yet, you must also know I will trust nothing you tell me."

Dr. Macpherson walked towards Lucifer, subtly interposing his body between the demon and Molly, though the latter didn't notice. "I had had the sense for some time that maybe you were annoyed at that business last year." Lucifer scowled, which Ross didn't acknowledge. "And now, I'm beginning to think I was right about that." He turned to Molly and winked. "And you said I wasn't good at dealing with people."

"I stand by that analysis," she said. "Like, this would never appear in the Williams' book on etiquette, even in one of the 'Getting It (Wr)On(g)' case study box outs."

"So you offer this woman as an apology? As if I need single souls like some simple succubus from the Pit?"

Dr. Macpherson laughed. "I hope you're a bit angrier at me than that," he said.

"When you die," Lucifer spoke calmly now, his words perfectly controlled and beautifully modulated as they exited his sensuous mouth, "I will come to Earth to collect your soul and for eternity your suffering will be so total that it will purge even the most wicked of their desire to sin."

"So you're saying you'll marry me?"

"You could do a lot worse, Ross," Molly said. "A man your age and with your looks has to start settling."

"My patience frays to its last thread," Lucifer said.

"What if I offered you a soul you wanted more than mine?" Dr. Macpherson said.

"There is none."

"What about the Blanched One," said Dr. Macpherson. "The vampire who has never tasted blood, and whose soul is as pure as the first snows on Everest."

"You fool," said Lucifer. "I have no claim on a stainless soul."

"You do not," said Dr. Macpherson. "But I have bound his soul to this woman's with the true cross and she is steeped in evil."

Lucifer stared at Molly, and his gaze seemed to blast through her with terrible force, shredding her to atoms and examining each with furious intelligence. "Her soul is rancid," he said. "And yes. I sense the link between her and Vampire Umpire."

"Wait, what?" Molly asked. "You can't mean...?" She turned to Dr. Macpherson and grabbed the lapels of his coat. "You said we were saving him. Now you're selling his soul to the devil?"

"Well no," said Dr. Macpherson. "That's not quite right. I'm also offering him yours."

"You bastard," she said, and swung her fist at his face. Swift as a tailor, he touched her hand with his finger and her arm hung numb beside her body. "How could you do this to him? You're his friend."

"I don't have friends," Ross said. She spat at him but he diverted the spittle to the side with a gesture of his hand. "Enough from you." His fingers made small strange gestures in the air, as if he were stringing it into a cat's cradle.

"I swear I will save him and kill you," Molly said, or tried to. But as she spoke the words seemed to coalesce in her throat and filled her mouth with a fine black ash, and she found herself falling to the ground and coughing the dust out onto the floor.

"So," Dr. Macpherson said. "My offer is simple: Vampire Umpire's soul I give to you and you relinquish any present and all future rights Hell might have to mine." Molly tried to kick him, but Lucifer held her away. She could feel tears of rage growing in the corners of her eyes, but refused to let them spill.

Contemplation dwelt in Lucifer's gaze. "The demons respect a soul like his," Ross said. "Since last year, is it not true that your power here is less total than it once was? Hell has a master and a mistress they say now, in the ice-carved halls of heaven. But with Vampire Umpire's soul as your war-standard, you can set aright the balance that now is swayed wrong."

All trace of thought was gone now. "I accept," Lucifer said. "And tonight I will collect his soul and see you on Earth."

◆

When they had left, Molly had resisted with all her strength, punching and kicking at Dr. Macpherson until finally he cast another spell, slaving her legs to his so that every step he took was echoed involuntarily by her. He had at least removed the spell that prevented her speech. "How could you?" she said, each word freighted with an almost unbearable sorrow.

"I just do my best," he said. "You know, you just go in with what you have, you negotiate and you see what happens. ABC is my guide: A always, B be, C charming. Always be charming."

"I hate you," she said. "And I swear I am going to stop this somehow."

She noticed they were not walking out of the city. Instead their path led deeper in. "Are you sure you won't talk to me?" Dr. Macpherson asked. "I always find conversation makes a long journey pass so much faster."

Molly kept silent. He seemed to feed on her insults, and she instead decided to think of a way out of this dilemma. They eventually arrived at a palace equal in scale to the first but carved instead of obsidian. As they entered, Molly saw that the palace was filled with spoiled meat, leaking blood and rot onto the bare floors. The walls swarmed with flies swollen and bloated and ripe, and no space was clear of their soft, undulating stridulations.

The symmetries of the two buildings was echoed in the central chamber, where a throne stood high but here empty. Dr. Macpherson knelt at the base of the throne and said, "Lilith, I seek an audience with the Queen of Hell."

From the dome above them a horde of flies swept down and formed on the throne into the rough shape of a woman. More and more flies joined the body until the entire form was replicated perfectly. The woman created thus would have been beautiful, if her every curve and feature had not been subtly writing with a slow flapping of translucent wings and the scuttle of tiny legs.

As Molly watched, the woman oozed forward and kissed Dr. Macpherson once on the lips. They conversed for a while in some language that might as well have been Greek to her, save for the two words Vampire Umpire that occurred once, and then Dr. Macpherson shook her hand, the demon handed him a bag of some kind, filled, Molly assumed, with mysterious secret treasures, and then they were leaving.

Together, silent, they walked out of Hell. Molly found herself weeping at the horrors she saw and the situation she had contrived. She had assumed that Dr. Macpherson's card had been in Vampire Umpire's bag for some good reason, and the man's quick response had further convinced her that there was some bond between the two. But in reality he had turned out to be a parasite just waiting to feast on her friend's momentary weakness. She would try to find some way to make things right, she thought, but right now her mind was as blank as a blackboard in a class taught by Betsy De Vos, and seemed every bit as hopeless.

♦

Back in the bedroom, Dr. Macpherson sat Molly down in a chair and opened the curtains. Night had fallen across Rome and the stars shone down over the terracotta roofs arrayed before him. He breathed in once and held it, then breathed out. He turned towards the bed and made a few sweeps in the air with his hands, uttering esoteric words as he did. Vampire Umpire writhed on the bed, and Molly knew the curse was killing him at last.

She had no plan, even now, and only one hope. When Lucifer arrived she would provoke Dr. Macpherson into talking and with luck he would say something that would so anger the King of Hell that she could renegotiate a deal. An eternity of pain would be sufficient for someone so faithless, she thought.

Not one but two portals opened in the room, and first Lucifer and then Lilith stepped through into the room.

"The King and Queen of Hell," Ross said, raising his arms in welcome. "I am so glad to have you both in my humble house."

"What is the meaning of this?" Lucifer asked.

"Oh don't you guys know?" Ross said. "I sold his soul to both of you, which means in," he checked his watch ostentatiously, "two minutes, when he dies, you are going to have to decide who gets the old thing."

♦

Had Molly spoken Greek, she would have heard the following conversation between Dr. Macpherson and Lilith.

Macpherson: I come to offer tribute to the Queen of Hell, and to suggest a bargain that could grant you dominion entire over all these lands.

Lilith: When you humiliated my husband, I made gains I would not mind extending.

Macpherson: And I who someday will dwell here would enjoy if Hell's ruler hated me a little less completely than the current owner/occupier.

Lilith: Speak then: what can you offer?

Macpherson: A pure soul, tied to the soiled one of this local and mute slattern with magics older than Christ. The one known as Vampire Umpire.

Lilith: His soul would sway the hosts of hell to back me entire. And what do you wish for granting me a kingdom? Life eternal? Riches?

Macpherson: The Light-bringer has reigned too long. Hell could use the gentler hand of the Queen of Radiant Night. And all I wish is that my soul be free of claim from any resident here.

Lilith: Granted, with pleasure.

Macpherson: And maybe a bag of M&Ms. I am hungry.

Lilith: That's fine too.

◆

"Y'know," Ross said. "One of the most important things in a marriage is communication, and I'm getting the sense you two need to work on that. I know a few decent counsellors, if you want a recommendation."

Lucifer grabbed Dr. Macpherson, plunging his fists deep into the skin of his torso and lifting him by his ribs, but the latter just shook his head. "I've halted the curse again," he said. "But if I die, Vampire Umpire dies too." Lucifer slowly lowered Ross down.

"In case that's not clear, Lilith, as I know your English isn't as fine as your Greek," he said, "Or her French, eh, Lucy?" he added with a wink. "When he dies, one of you two will need to claim his soul. The soul that basically will grant whoever gets it the true throne of Hell."

"Another trick," Lucifer said. "So then we shall leave, and you can sustain him with your magic. When you die, one of us will take your foul soul and the other his, and equality will be maintained."

"If either of you leave, I release the spell and he dies," Dr. Macpherson said.

"So then what? Do you wish merely to bring Hell to war with itself?" Lilith asked.

"The alternative," Ross said, and finally Molly saw what his aim had been all along, "is that one of you lift the curse. I will then undo the binding of his soul and we can all just walk away from this."

Lilith and Lucifer glanced at each other, and Lilith stepped back through her portal, which closed behind her. A few flies trailing behind her were left, and they collapsed to the floor and rotted away.

Lucifer reached inside Vampire Umpire's flesh, though his fingers left no mark and caused no wound. When he removed his hand, the curse was in his fingers, where it danced around like a ferret coiling around a beloved owner's leg. "Undo your spells, wizard," he said.

"When you leave," Ross said.

Lucifer stared coldly at Ross. "Your life is an eyeblink to me," he said. "And whether it is the indignities of feeble old age or one of your enemies that takes you, you will belong to me," he promised.

"And if I lived as long as you," Ross said. "Maybe one day you would be the one getting the best of me. Get lost, mate: I'm done with you." He casually tossed the true cross fragment at Lucifer's face. The strike knocked the demon back into the portal with tremendous force and burned a mark into that previously pristine flesh. "A memento, until I do die," Ross added. Then, working his spell, he slammed the portal closed.

♦

Vampire Umpire stirred on the bed. Molly ran to him, and was holding his hand and staring into his eyes when he woke. "How am I not dead?" he said.

"Oh," said Molly. "Gosh. Don't you remember? You are dead."

Vampire Umpire's eyes widened and Molly continued, "You're a vampire, remember?"

"Ohhhh, good one. Makes me wish I were actually dead, so I didn't have to hear it," he said.

"Rude," said Molly. "We just went through Hell to save you, pretty much literally."

"You'll be weak for a few days," Ross said. "And Molly: that sap from Hell's trees will wash clean in a week or so. Your soul will be dark until then, so maybe stay out of churches if you don't like bursting into flame. Oh, one second." He chanted for a moment and Molly felt the soul binding he had done before loosen. She felt simultaneously lighter but also more alone. "That's everything, I think," he said. "I'll leave you guys to get reacquainted."

He stepped out into the living room, and after a moment Molly followed. She wasn't sure where to begin, the cruelty and thoughtlessness of his manner almost outweighing the selflessness he had exhibited in his deeds. But when she entered the room she saw another portal closing, this one opening onto a greener, more pleasant place than Hell – somewhere, she sensed also, not in America but somewhere pleasant on Earth – and the magician was gone, never to be seen by her again, which I promise is true, you can keep reading.

She walked back through to Vampire Umpire's bedroom. "He's left," she said.

"Yeah, that's his way," Vampire Umpire said. "He does what he feels is right but he hates being thanked."

"I can't say I like him, but he did save you."

"I'm his friend," Vampire Umpire said.

"He said he doesn't have friends."

"He doesn't," said Vampire Umpire. "Just me. He's an unlikeable man, until you really get to know him, which no-one ever does and as a result he's the loneliest person I know. But he will give everything in the service of what he believes is right." Molly looked sceptical. "I mean he's no role medal," he added hastily.

"Role *medal?*"

"Yeah, like someone so admirable you want to hang them around your neck to remind you of their courage and goodness?"

Molly looked deeply sceptical, but continued, "I guess that could be how that phrase is said. Well he did his work tonight, but I'm glad he's gone."

"Like getting the runs after a big Mexican meal?" Vampire Umpire asked.

"Exactly like that, in every possible way."

Chapter Thirteen

To be fair to the Pope, Molly thought, it was pretty justifiable that he was so angry she had lost the only extant piece of the true cross. As he screamed at her, as his holy spittle flecked her face like a particularly wet baptism, she just tried to remember that Vampire Umpire was okay and waiting at home for her. At length, a wad of spit went in her eye and she said, "Pipe down, Popey. I've seen possessed babies hock up less than you."

The Pope hesitated in his tirade, fascinated by this latest facet of the tennis player he had so grown to admire. "You have much experience with exorcisms?" he asked.

"Umm, no, I was really just referring to the movie and to the fact that children are, among their other bad features, pretty much just trailing spit wherever they go, like snails only even more disgusting," she said. "And they have horrid dirty hands, like in a DH Lawrence novel but with none of the repressed sexuality and only some of the barely concealed fascism."

"Basically the reason I became pope was to ensure I never had any kids," the Pope said. "I mean I like the ladies just fine, but

I don't want to plant any seeds. I don't want extra mouths I can't feed."

"I hear that," Molly said and held out her fist to bump with his.

"Don't hit me!" the Pope said, cowering.

"Noo," she said. "It's like this." She made him put out his fist and she lightly bumped it with her own, before pulling it back and making a little "lulululu" sound and waggling her opened fingers.

"I love it!" the Pope said. "This is going to work so much better than the papal salute."

"Yeah, you can use it," she said. "I like to think I'm an influencer."

"You are," the Pope said. "What with this and the outtie 5000 thing, you have shaped the catholic church more than anyone since the first council of Nicaea."

"Noice," she said. "I take a pretty mean selfie if you want to put my picture on any of your money or stained glass windows."

"Send some to my email address please. It is godmale@hotmail.com."

"Man I bet you get a lot of spam."

"Yeah, mainly from hopeful homosexual men," the Pope said. "That mailbox has had more D in it than Taylor Swift."

"BLASPHEMY!" Molly shouted, and struck the Pope across the head, knocking his hat to the ground.

"I'm sorry!" the Pope said. "I will also work on my previous slut shaming, which an astute observer might consider as a synecdoche for the inherent sexism of the catholic church, which you have also helped to change."

"So am I now more influential that the first council of Nikita or whatever?"

"Probably, yes," the Pope said.

"So a good start to the day," said Molly. "Okay Popey, I have to go to my tennis final now."

♦

A few days had passed since her journey to Hell, and Vampire Umpire was slowly recovering his strength. Since he slept during the day, a deep sleep so close to death that it and death would probably have been going steady or at the very least doing under the clothes stuff on the sly, Molly had kept attending the tournament and, as far as she could tell, winning matches. In any case, they didn't seem surprised each day when she turned up and played, so either they were being very polite or she was winning.

Today when she stepped up to the net, she found Jebediah Moslius waiting for her. He was dressed head to toe in black, branded in white with the logo he had had designed for him – a J and an M in ornate uncial script, with the lines of the letters traced into the lines of a tennis ball. She noticed the same design on a double finger bar ring he wore, made of creamy gold and studded with a large diamond at the centre of each letter.

"Hey man," she said. "Let's try to get this over quickly, okay? I want to go to the movies this afternoon."

"This is one of the most prestigious tournaments in the world," Moslius protested. "When I won it last year, I spent an entire week on a yacht in the med, sucking champagne out of the dimples in the backs of three models."

"Hand models, right?"

"Full body models!"

"So prostitutes," Molly said knowingly, and shook her head. "For shame."

Moslius kicked furiously at the red clay of the court, digging a deep divot. The umpire walked over to them. "If you're ready, we can do the coin toss and the pictures," he said, smoothing out the displaced court with his foot.

Molly lost the coin toss, so Moslius chose to serve first. Molly tied her hair back into a pony tail so it wouldn't get in her face during the match. She didn't usually worry about that, but it was a hot day, and she wanted to see if she could cool herself by frisking it about, like a horse did. She and Moslius stood on opposite sides of the net and faced the thicket of cameras bristled by both the crowd and the more professional photographers, by which I mean the photographers who were paid for taking photos, not that the crowd were behaving childishly or engaging in any antics or schemes.

Moslius clasped her hand as hard as he could, clearly trying to hurt her and assert dominance. She was fine with it, having hands stronger than the foundations of the earth, but suddenly he went, "Jeesus, why are your fingers so wet?"

She thought back and realised she must have picked something up when she passed them through her hair. "Ohhh, that's pope spit," she explained.

This was why, in the photos of the match later run on websites and newspapers all over the world, Molly is standing smiling pleasantly at the cameras while beside her, Jebediah Moslius is frantically trying to pull his hand from out of her grip and looks like he is simultaneously crying and about to vomit, an emotion now defined as cromitting.

They moved to their correct positions on the court shortly after, Molly (as always) being slightly directed in this by the staff surrounding them, and the match commenced.

◆

Forty minutes later, the tournament director was handing Molly the trophy. "Congratulations," she said to Molly. "You joined the tennis tour this year, and so far you have a perfect win record: how does that feel?"

"Doesn't everyone have a perfect win record?" Molly asked. "Other than, y'know, the people I play, I guess?"

"No, very few people on the tour will win more than 10 matches total this year. You've won 40 already. In fact, the only person close to you is Moslius, who has only three losses, all to you?"

"Really? I thought he was one of the worst players I played. In both manners and ability." At this point the commentator looked over awkwardly at Moslius, who was standing holding the plate awarded to the player who came second.

"Ummm, no, in fact he is still according to the rankings the number one player in the world."

"According to the rankings?" Moslius yelled. "What the hell does that mean?" He threw the plate on the ground, and around the stadium the crowd began to boo. Moslius stomped off the court, while the director watched and then, trying to save the situation, continued.

"Though as more tournaments pass, you gain more and more points, so maybe you will finish the year as number one, eh? Achieving that must have been a lifelong dream?"

"Not really," said Molly. "I mean, if it happens it happens, but the only lifelong dream I have is that one where I'm hiding in a cupboard from a monster and it's in the room and I'm trying so hard not to breathe I have my hands clamped over my mouth and then all my teeth start falling out and rattling on the floor and the monster opens the door." She paused and breathed. "It's a lot of pressure to deal with."

"Well quite. So you're the champion of Rome's Masters Tennis Tournament, on an incredible streak this year with many calling you the greatest of all time: how do you feel?"

Molly thought, then leaned over towards the microphone. "I mean, a little hungry. I guess I should have had breakfast but I had a busy morning. And I'm looking forward to going to the movies later and I can probably get a snack there, even though it's a bit expensive."

"Thanks a lot," the director said, and once again abandoned Molly to bob around on the sea of admiration in which the crowd drowned her.

◆

In the penthouse office of the tennis federation in Rome, Tyrone Ennis stood in front of Jean and Ham Remington, frowning furiously. "Yet another of my umpires has been attacked," he said. "And neither of you have made any progress in finding the culprit."

"We're doing our best," Jean said, while simultaneously Ham was saying, "I just feel too sad to investigate: like isn't the real victim here my broken heart?"

Fortunately, Tyrone Ennis heard only Jean's statement. "I just want my personnel to be safe. Vampire Umpire will be fine, thankfully, and he will return to umpiring at our next tournament. But if you can't find out who the vampire is soon, maybe Vampire Umpire won't survive the next attack, and other than him often getting sick in the mornings so he can only umpire at night, he's the best umpire I have on tour."

"Plus he's just a super likeable guy," Ham said.

"So nice," said Jean. "I'm honestly shocked anyone would even be able to harm him."

"Oh he's a real gem of a person," Tyrone Ennis agreed. "Listen, I'm sorry for getting on at you. But please do your best, okay?"

Both Jean and Ham agreed, and Tyrone Ennis, who was one of the most gifted managers in the world, rewarded them with the delicious scones he had hidden for that very purpose in the room.

◆

After the movies, Molly went home, where Vampire Umpire was awake in bed reading a large novel. "What're you reading?" she asked.

"Oh, it's Against the Day, by Thomas Pynchon," he replied.

"Any good?"

"It's very disappointing. I assumed from the title it would be a book about how day really sucks, especially when compared to the night."

"When *you* really suck," Molly added.

"But it turns out it is just an impossibly brilliant literary novel about the explosive development of technology in the 20th century and how it essentially bifurcated the world into one where science fantasy and scientific reality became almost indistinguishable."

"Yeah, I don't care about any of that."

"How was the tournament?" he asked.

"Oh, I won. But the movie was amazing." She described the plot and dialogue at length, deviating in her description only several times to praise the deliciousness of the popped corns she had enjoyed.

"It sounds good," he said. "When I'm better I might have seen it, if you hadn't basically just acted all of it out for me."

"So if anything you've got to experience it for free and better, because it was acted by me?" Molly asked.

"Exactly," he said.

Molly stared at Vampire Umpire, still looking weak after his ordeal, and felt in her stomach that same vertiginous fear you got when you stood looking down a sheer cliff even while holding the barrier that prevented you from falling: the sense of terrible events held back by something too fragile. "Vampire Umpire," she said. "Is it true what Dr. Macpherson said? Have you never drunk on human blood?"

"I mean, occasionally, when one of my girlfriends has been surfing the red tide," he said, and winked.

"Gross," she said. "You sicken me."

"Okay, no, I haven't," Vampire Umpire admitted.

"But how do you survive?" she asked.

"Vampires are undead," he said. "We don't need food like you do, for energy or survival. The blood... whatever it is that drives us, for no-one knows, it calls out for blood like a true heart aches for the person it most loves." He hesitated, "No, it's not as clean or pure as that: the hunger dwells within all vampires like an addiction and it gnaws and screams within always unless quieted with blood."

"So every moment, you feel all of that and you just... ignore it?" He nodded. "You'd be an *amazing* baby sitter."

"You get used to it in time," he said. "And obviously I have had centuries of it."

"Will you tell me about it?" she asked.

"If you like."

"Tell me now," she said, sitting down in the chair beside the bed, which she turned to face him.

"You're sure you don't want some…"

"Hold on," she interrupted him, leaping out of the chair. "Let me get some snacks first."

Chapter Fourteen

I never knew the names of either of my parents. I have only hazy impressions of them, like looking at a Monet painting through a fog. I only know three things. They were farmers who grew primarily organic kale, which they attempted to sell for inflated prices at local markets, believing it would provide extra protein if added to something they called juices. Sadly, as juices had yet to be invented they were too far ahead of their time to make a profit, like Giammbatista Canopener, who invented the can opener fifteen centuries before the discovery of tin technology. They lived sometime in the middle ages. And for reasons I cannot adumbrate they named me Vampire Umpire.

Sadly, much like juices, prophylactics had also not been invented, and when I was just beginning to walk and speak and work a fourteen-hour day on the farm hoeing weeds out of the kale with my shucking device much like a prostitute hoes the seeds out of the males with their fucking so nice, my mother's womb kindled with another child. My sister was born with the spring rains, and I know not if her tears or the heavens' wet the ground more.

Since the farm failed to support us at all, this being also before the invention of an economy so that people had to bind together into communities or just be self-sufficient, making my parents' business even less viable, having a second child was really stretching it. My parents decided, as any would in their situation, to design a series of contests to determine who was the mightier child and thus kept and who was a big sad loser and should be given away.

I had always been a daydreamer, though, and one day while weeding the kale innocently and absent-mindedly, I remember my father sprinting over the field towards me bellowing incoherent threats. I had somehow managed to hoe the entire kale field completely bare – bare like the sweet cupboard in a scotch man's house, not bear like a hairy fat man who enjoys homosexual congress – and I had etched into the earth a series of squares and rectangles in some curious design.

Having destroyed their livelihood in one swift afternoon and possibly doomed them to a slow death from kale withdrawal, my parents abandoned both the whole idea of a contest, and also me in a nearby town. I was unused to the crowds and the noise of great metropolises, and this one contained multitudes – more than fifteen people dwelt within.

Unable to deal with seeing sixteen people every day, I almost went mad with fear. For a couple of weeks, I lived on the town garbage pile, where I was adopted by a couple of friendly rats. Each night the rats would kiss my eyes as I fell asleep. Sometimes they got a bit toothy, but some people just kiss like that, and I would just gently push them away and a few days later the bleeding would usually stop.

One night when I slept I dreamt of some far-distant place blossoming in the spring, when the trees are not yet full with foliage and glow with both beauty and the beauty yet to come, like a glimpse into a future gravid with life. There was a lawn of grass as green as apples still on the tree and soft as a rat's underbelly fur pressed over your mouth while you slept as it tried to chew through your throat. Lines were etched into the grass in white, lines that matched the ones I had drawn while destroying my parents' farm. And two figures at opposite ends struck some kind of orb back and forth to each other, moving with such athleticism and skill it was dazzling to behold. I twisted and turned watching the flight of the orb and though the dream lasted for hours I still counted it too short.

But when I woke I found that my motions in the realm of Morpheus had translated into movement of my corporeal body. My back was wet and sticky, and I found I had crushed my rat-mother and rat-father and thoroughly exsanguinated them. Once again, my thoughtless and brutal actions had lead to me being orphaned. I buried my foster rodents under a pile of particularly nice garbage and wept over their graves for a few moments.

My grief had quenched my fear, and I set off into the streets. It was not long before a travelling alchemist stopped me. He had silvery white hair in a widow's peak and an angular face that expressed itself most forcefully in a nose like a hatchet.

"Who are you, girl?" he asked me, my hair having grown long during my time of neglect and the oils of the garbage dump making it shine like a rat's fangs under the moon as it charged your face because of night hunger. "Are you the burgomaster's new wife?"

This was an earlier time, when people married younger and taking a bride of perhaps five or six years of age was considered thrifty bargaining as you'd probably get twenty-five to thirty years out of them before they died, as opposed to now when attempting to marry someone that age would get you twenty-five to thirty years in jail or just death. Also a burgomaster was the master of a burg, meaning town: not someone who was just really good at cooking burgers.

I answered him no and corrected him as to my gender, then told him of my life as a monstrous child who wreaked destruction in his wake like a particularly selfish Godzilla.

"In truth Vampire Umpire," he said, "I was most taken by the colour of your shirt." The rat's blood had turned the dirty fabric of my shirt a vivid red, and I did look pretty swagadocious, as people of the time said. That was a portmanteau of the words "swag" and braggadocio, and had the writers of the blogosphere existed then and had writing been commonly distributed and cheap, I would have topped many a "Hot List" with ease with my on-point styles.

The alchemist, Nicolas Flamel, made me an offer then. He made his living by bartering cures and remedies for food, but he also was renowned for his unusual dyes. I would join him on his journeys from town to town, and he would train me in the ways of alchemy if he could have my shirt to attempt to replicate the a la mode colour that would so wow, he believed, "the ladieeez".

Of course I agreed, and so commenced the next phase of my life. For many years we made a circuit around Europe, and Flamel was welcomed in town squares as small as a postage stamp as warmly as in courts where Kings and Queens sought his counsel. At his instruction I learned first the techniques to fashion ingredients: how to dry or otherwise prepare herbs, how to grind minerals into appropriately fine levels of powder. Then it was combining ingredients.

As my skill grew he began to tell me the correct recipes to make many of his concoctions, and for a good few years many of Flamel's Cure All Tinctures had been produced entirely without any efforts from the great alchemist himself.

I was almost full grown when he began to teach me the last of the arts of alchemy – glassblowing. Many potions require the precipitation of salts or the fine extraction of vapours and not for no reason did Flamel always sleep with his alembic chest for a pillow. He showed me how to prepare the sand and how to heat the furnace, and how to turn the glass so it formed properly and true.

I picked up the skill quickly and I displayed quite the knack, Flamel said. Glassblowing was an expensive process, and when Flamel needed a new vessel made he soon trusted me more than himself. One day he asked for a complete new set, having found a journeyman alchemist to whom he could sell his increasingly worn equipment. He left me to work for a day and a night with much of his fortune spent on the raw materials he entrusted to my care and skill.

When he returned the next day, though, he soon discovered how foolish his trust had been. Once again, my idée fixe had taken hold. I had filled every shelf in the room with perfectly round orbs, in likeness identical to the one in my dream. Like them they were decorated around their equator with an odd undulating design, that wended around the surface sinuously.

He was ruined, he believed, though I later discovered he managed to sell the orbs to a local tribe of Romany gypsies as something he called an "Orb of Thesulah" and doubled his fortune. Our partnership was entirely dissolved though, and had his words not been clear, the thorough and vicious beating he delivered with a long oak staff certainly conveyed his meaning adequately.

Thankfully this time I was not an innocent child abandoned. I had useful skills and knowledge and I before long I was also well known as a trustworthy alchemist, though I took care to avoid any town where I might meet my former master. One year I was walking through Romania and I passed a night in a small hamlet. I stayed in a young, poor farmer's house. His name was Hamlet, and poor nutrition had given him no length of bone. His mother was sick with what we would now term pneumonia, and though I knew they could not spare any food for me as recompense, I gave them such tinctures as would be effective.

The next morning when I left the son thanked me, and he gave me some advice. "It would be a poor choice to go into the mountains," he said, "for there are those there who you would not wish to meet. You'll be cursed if you head that way, for sure."

Well naturally I assumed he meant what anyone would assume: that the people of the mountains had never encountered an alchemist before and would not be interested in my services. But of course there he was simply showing his ignorance of business, as would be expected of a simple farmer: if anything the scarcity of alchemists would create demand for their services and drive prices up.

I set off into the mountains. On the first night I had to make camp in a small clearing. I heard wolves howl somewhere distant but too close for my repose to be perfect, and in the night I woke several times and seemed to see red eyes gazing at me from the flickering shadows cast by my fire on the trees bounding the edge of the clearing. But the next morning, sure enough, I immediately encountered a village where I was able to sell all my goods for high prices. But I did strain my back slightly, after my night sleeping rough and from having to carry the heavy weight of all that gold, so perhaps the farmer had been write to caution me.

I needed to gather new ingredients so I headed to Bucharest, which was the nearest city. The journey was long, and unfortunately that night I made the terrible decision to stop at a small local castle on the outskirts of the city. The lord who greeted me at the door had a great mane of grey hair so fine it looked as if his head was garlanded with cobwebs that for centuries had caught only dust. His skin was cracked with age and his lips were pale and bloodless.

"I bid you enter," he told me. "Though it has been… long since any have known my hospitality."

He disappeared into the castle after situating me in the dining hall. After a long while he returned with a hastily made stew and a dust-coated bottle of wine, which he opened by piercing the cork with one of his long, taloned nails. He poured me a glass. "Are you not having?" I asked.

"I never drink… wine," he said.

Throughout dinner he watched me eat with an avidity I found disconcerting, and when he led me to my bedchamber, he lingered in the door way. "I would not wander tonight," he said. "This castle has many... dangers that could claim the unwary."

I lay down to sleep, and I am sure you know what comes next in my sad and tragic story. The bed was poorly fashioned, the mattress lumpy, and the sheets coarser than a dock worker from Essex, and my sleep gave me an odd pain in my neck that didn't fully dispel until the afternoon of the next day.

I was in the city by then and a very small proportion of what I had made in the mountains resupplied me completely. So I decided that night to treat myself to a stay in a good inn, with beds that were as soft as fontanel.

That night the nobleman next door came into my room to chat to me. "S'up dude," he said, or something that meant roughly the same but was not so anachronistic.

"Not much, you?" I replied and we discoursed through a number of hours. It turned out he was the son of the lord in whose castle I had just passed my night of horrors. The castle, he informed me, was quite dilapidated, and wanderers often found themselves falling down crumbling staircases or through floors grown rotten with poor maintenance. The man's father had squandered his fortune during a past where he had entangled himself too thoroughly in the vine, and since, though he had foresworn all drink, could not afford repairs.

The son had spent many years at war in Turkey and had accumulated a new fortune by his feats of arms. The next night he intended to return to his father's home and restore the family to greatness. "Why tomorrow night?" I asked him. "Why not just go in the morning?"

"My father is how old would you say?"

"Aww man," I replied, "your father's so old all of his childhood friends are extinct because they were dinosaurs." Of course at the time, these creatures were known as saurians of the earth, but I modernised the name to make the joke land.

"He is one hundred and fifteen, and he had me when he was thirty."

The man looked to be only in his late twenties, so I expressed disbelief at this claim, as politely as I could, for this was still in the times when a rich person could murder a commoner and instead of being censured be rewarded for it. Actually that is still true, ignore that clarification.

"Oh right, that's why I was subtly questioning you. I forgot to mention in my story, but I'm a vampire," he said. "I just assumed with you being called Vampire Umpire that you were also a vampire."

I had no clue what that was, but I found out fast, because he basically immediately seized me in his mighty fists and bent my head back and plunged his long canine teeth into my neck.

The next night I woke and he explained to me that because he'd enjoyed talking to me he had decided not to kill me and instead to make me a vampire like him. He explained the hunger I felt then, the need for blood that gripped me the way an addict lusts for their drug of choice.

That first night, when he selected a victim for me in the streets, guided her into the alley in which I waited and watched from afar, I knew I would never drink blood. First because it's gross: it goes to everywhere in the body, and that includes the bum. And also, because I had never had the desire to take advantage of someone for my benefit, which is probably why I have never held a political post.

Lucas, the nobleman vampire, took me with him to his father's castle that night, and we spent many years restoring it. He wasn't too fussed about me not drinking blood, much as you would not be concerned if a friend chose to be vegetarian. After all, it's not like they're vegans and therefore dicks. We had many adventures together, and I had many more on my own. There was my battle with the cannibal cult in Budapest, the time I prevented the rise of an ancient evil god, which had slept for centuries in a temple in the Phillipines before a volcanic eruption woke it. Almost as memorable was my time as an opera singer in Paris, or my successful hunt for Jack the Ripper. My crusade against the Luftwampir Women of the SS in World War 2 is still spoken off in many quarters of the military with awe. But all of those pale next to the most significant moment of my life, and moreover would be more at home in a sequel or collection of linked short stories, possibly issued by a high end luxury press, maybe given the title FANGS FOR THE MEMORIES, because it would all be flashbacks.

It was 1873 and I was in an estate in England visiting friends, when I saw a green grass court, laid out in the pattern I had drawn as a child. Under arc lamps bought at vast expense, two men darted about, striking a ball in exactly the way I had foreseen. And that was how I discovered tennis and knew I wanted to be an umpire, for with my vampire skills, competing would spoil the game the way doping does other sports. Umpiring, however, would allow me to take part and in a way that enhanced it: for with my delicate senses there would be no wrong line calls or bad judgements. In all the long years after, I struggled to realise that dream, and now I finally have. And so centuries of life as a vampire finally let me witness the sport I had dreamed of as a child, and take part in it in the small way in which I am able.

◆

"And that is the story," said Vampire Umpire, "of how I discovered tennis."

"I mean it certainly was long," she said. "I'm not going to lie, I skipped a lot of it."

"And what of you, Molly?"

"What do you mean?"

"Why do you play tennis? It is obvious you have no real interest in it, just an insane natural skill."

Molly shrugged. "I had a boyfriend a while back. I didn't like him all that much, but he was okay, and he loved tennis. He was also a diabetic."

"So a sweet guy?"

"Ha." Molly shrugged again. "One day he was visiting a candy factory when his blood sugar went low. He reached into one of the tubs of molten chocolate, trying to get some sugar so he wouldn't pass out. But the turbine that stirs the chocolate was passing and snared his hand and pulled him in."

"Oh that's awful," Vampire Umpire said.

Molly continued, her eyes unblinking so she would not show any emotion. "Nobody noticed he was missing though, and the turbine slowly tore his body to shreds like someone ripping apart boiled chicken with a fork. The candy bars resulting from it were sold all over the UK and were so popular that the company in question is looking for suicidal diabetics so they can establish it as a regular variety of their product."

"I... see."

"Yeah. So as a memorial to him, I decided to play a tennis match, and I started winning and making serious money," she said.

"And?" said Vampire Umpire.

"And I figured out if I can win every tournament I will have enough money to buy that company and shut them down," she said. "Or maybe just share the profits. I figure those bars are gonna make hella benjamins."

Vampire Umpire looked at Molly and she felt no-one had ever beheld her with more pride or admiration.

Chapter Fifteen

Molly walked up the gangplank onto the ship dragging the wooden trunk behind her, causing an extremely loud squeaking sound and scraping twin gouges into the previously pristine deck where the joints of the trunk met the ground. "Yeah," she yelled belligerently, "just my tennis equipment. I'm definitely not smuggling anyone on board hidden in this extremely unusually heavy case." The ship was an ocean liner called the *Terrible Love*. Vampire Umpire had recovered a lot of his strength in the past few days, but they had been unable to find a flight that would definitely land in New York in the night time, so they had booked passage on the ship instead. It would take six days to cruise out of the Mediterranean, all across the Atlantic and dock in the harbour and, Molly thought, that assumed none of the guests wanted to pause to do a little light whaling.

Two porters offered to help with her trunk but she didn't want them knowing how heavy it was and getting suspicious, so she continued pulling it herself. After all, it wasn't the first occasion when she had had to vigorously yank around a really large thing for a long time.

She was just entering the cabin deck backwards, kicking back hard with her left leg to open the door when she heard a loud crunching sound, and an English accent from one of the posher regions of that country saying, "Good lord, I'm absolutely positive my nose is broken and even should that prove not to be the case, I am in tremendous pain."

A woman spoke next. Her accent was indeterminate, containing sounds of many countries, but she spoke beautifully when she said, "I'm a bit more concerned about my dress. It's white, and you've now got it all bloody. It's rather calling to mind the bed sheet after a medieval wedding."

"Cecily, I do wish you would not say things like that. Anyone could hear us."

"Well, gee whiz George, it's not like we're going at it. Just try to relax would you?"

Molly pushed the door open, using her hand this time, and peered around. "Oh, are you okay?" she asked, the man. He had a crown of grey hair fringing his scalp and a goatee of the same colour, though now artificially highlighted by twin rivulets of blood trickling down from each nostril. "One of the sailors just kicked the door hard and ran off. He said something about the door trying to, um, steal his boyfriend, but I didn't catch all of it."

"It does have a pretty nice porthole," Cecily said, winking at her subtly. She was perhaps in her sixties, though she had an ageless quality that made that hard to judge, and she did wear a white dress on which a few specks of blood had landed, as if she were a snowfield in a Quentin Tarantino film. She was wearing a sunhat, with a pair of Ray Ban sunglasses resting neatly on the brim, emerald earrings set in gold, and a pair of white gloves that stretched to just about her wrist. "Cecily Cholmondeley," she said. "This man is George St. Drake, my companion on this trip." She tapped him on the elbow. "Go find the medical office, George," she spoke louder to him, as if trying to make her instructions extra clear. "We need to stop up that blood flow, and I haven't had to carry around tampons for about twenty years."

George walked off, into the maze of corridors in the body of the ship and Cecily waited about five femtoseconds before continuing, "And not my companion for any longer than the voyage lasts, thankfully."

"You're not together?"

"Goodness, no," Cecily said and patted Molly's arm lightly. "I met him in a bar in Istanbul before getting on the ship and he told me he'd just found out that his travel agent hadn't secured him a birth. So I thought it was a sign." She sighed. "Of course, the only sign it was was that George is so terribly boring his poor travel agent probably fell asleep while trying to listen to him."

"It did seem like anywhere in the world would be a lot more tolerable with him not in it," Molly said.

"Well quite," Cecily said. "So thank you very much for slamming that door into his face."

"I mean, I wish I'd known he was there beforehand, so I could do it deliberately," Molly said, "but that is my one regret."

"Can I help you? Return the favour, if only a little bit?"

Cecily held the door open while Molly hauled through her luggage. "Thanks," she said.

"No worries. I'm going to hide in the bar now, behind enough emptied martini glasses that George won't find me 'til dinner time. Once you're unpacked, you're welcome to join me."

◆

Their cabin was like a galaxy: extremely spacious and filled with fancy shiny things that Molly had little clue about other than a healthy reluctance to touch them. There were two king-size beds, swaddled in enough sheets to cover all the tables the Queen owned but didn't want to either use or get dust on. A large balcony, on which Romeo would have able to court a Juliet of tremendous size, looked down onto the ocean far below, where Molly saw a pod of dolphins following. She spat over the side, aiming for the blowhole of the lead dolphin and believed she hit it dead centre. Certainly it sprayed out a cloud of some kind of material, hopefully in disgust, and the pod fell back.

While the dolphin was regularly portrayed as the friendly idiot of the seas, like an aqua-based golden retriever or a forrest gump that had somehow mastered scuba gear despite his dim-witted ways, it was in fact one of the few animals that both reproduced through gang rape and killed the babies that resulted, sometimes after using them for an impromptu game of volleyball. They were also riddled with STDs, which was by far the main reason to worry about getting some dolphin in your tuna. Every sane person should hate dolphins, the college freshmen of the seas.

She went into the bathroom, where the only feature not clad in gold was the silver of the large mirror. Even the toilet seat had some filigree, and she momentarily recalled her long-standing desire to break into Fort Knox, the United States gold reserve, and just whiz everywhere, making it a double golden stockpile.

The afternoon sun streamed in the cabin window like a youtube personality with tremendously high bandwidth. The air seemed almost freighted with liquid light of rich orange hue and pleasant warmth. Unfortunately, that meant opening the case was probably not a great idea, so she could do no unpacking.

She lay on one of the beds for a moment and found a remote for a television, though no television was visible in the room. She pushed the on button and a previously seamless section of the wall slid down and in and a large television appeared in its place. Unfortunately only three channels were available: Dave, which showed a series of dramatic readings of the postmodern novelist David Foster Wallace by David Attenborough sitting on a stool, the readings occasionally intercut with long moments of Attenborough sobbing for water or begging for a comfier chair; Animal Planet, which it turned out showed only videos of poor people of the inner city, with a sneering commentary where one of the stars of Made in Chelsea said, "Look at this poor scum here," each time a new video was introduced; and Bravo, which showed only finely staged operas. The realm of the rich was a vain, wicked, foolish place, full of all sort of humbugs and falsenesses and pretensions.

She decided to join Cecily in the bar, assuming she could find it, and left Vampire Umpire a note on the cabin's stationery, telling him where she would be and how thoroughly she hoped to have tied one on for when he woke.

♦

Vampire Umpire walked into the bar a brace of hours later. As always, he was dressed either like the kind of person who might be on trial for some barely to be encompassed financial crime, or someone about to be buried by a family who liked them well enough that they weren't going to just bundle them into the ground in a t-shirt with their genitals swaddled in a supermarket's (in this case) ironically named bag-for-life.

"Is this your friend?" Cecily asked Molly. The pile of emptied glasses would probably have caused a moderate sized eclipse, and most by far belonged to the older woman.

"That's him," Molly said. "Vampire Umpire!" she shouted, even though he was already heading over.

"He's very handsome," Cecily was saying. "If I were twenty years younger, I'd definitely be throwing my hat into the ring for him." She paused for a moment and thought, then added, "And also my knickers."

"Ha! If anything, you're too young for him," Molly said.

Vampire Umpire sat down next to Molly, and placed a martini glass in front of each of the women. He sipped his own elegantly, prefacing each swallow with a neat little turn to the stem of the glass. Molly introduced them, and the group spoke together happily until the bell sounded to announce it was time to dress for dinner.

"How the hell did you afford this?" Molly asked him, back in their ludicrously luxurious cabin. She had needed to change out of the jeans and T-shirt she had been wearing previously, as the T-shirt had the slogan "You bone it, you own it." Vampire

Umpire was also changing into, as far as Molly could tell, an exactly as fancy looking suit. "Are you selling naked pictures of me online?"

"Please!" Vampire Umpire said. "I have other sources of income, you know. That's just the most lucrative."

"I'm like a dyslexic trying to buy glasses," Molly said. "Getting sceptical."

"Actually the room was free to me," said Vampire Umpire, "as the captain is a friend of mine. Ship captains in general love to have a vampire on-board. We get a free voyage and in return we use our vampire rat control powers to keep away all the rats."

"Really? I thought usually captains were terrified of vampires. What about that whole Whitby/Demeter thing?"

"Oh, a total misunderstanding! You see the quartermaster of the Demeter had sold most of the ship's food to pay off his debt at the local brothel, and so when the captain had the possibly trademarked vampire in question scare away the rats, there was no food for the passengers and almost everyone starved."

"I'm learning a lot about nautical matters," Molly said. "And I like it."

"We'll make a seaman out of you yet," Vampire Umpire said.

"Only if we get out of this cabin soon," Molly said. "It's too hot and if I stay here much longer I am going to be a hot, melted pile of seaman."

♦

Molly and Vampire Umpire sat down at the captain's table. Captain Jessica Aubrey sat them to her left. To the right of her were Cecily Cholmondeley and George St. Drake. "Good evening," Captain Aubrey said, "and welcome to the ship. Do you all know each other?" There was a series of exchanges about who knew whom, but in practice it would not be interesting to read and would occupy about two hundred and fifty now deleted words of little benefit to the reader's wisdom or humour.

St. Drake occupied the captain with a discussion of ocean currents, which he insisted on pronouncing "ji-rez" even though the word was spelled and pronounced gyres. The general thrust of his argument was the idea that climate change should be accelerated so that the North Atlantic drift would cease, and rich people would be able to travel faster south in their yachts since they would no longer have to beat back against the current.

Molly said, sotto voce, to Vampire Umpire, "I'm going to ask her in a minute."

"Ask her what?"

'Adoy! If I can have a go on the wheel."

"What?"

"I was thinking about that seamen thing earlier," Molly said, at which moment Cecily's attention was fully captured, as the ejaculation of seaman or any of its homophones was often stimulating to her interest. "And I feel like I'd like to have a go on the ship."

"This is a six-hundred-million-dollar boat," Vampire Umpire whispered back. "She's not going to let you 'have a go" on it."

"Nahh, nah, nah," Molly assured him. "I'll do it real subtle-like."

The captain was just finishing some sentence of which they only caught the end: "monstrous cataclysm that might destroy all humanity." Molly tapped on her arm, and Aubrey's attention swung to her more tolerable guests.

"Hey captain," Molly said. "I'd love to have a go on the wheel."

"Nailed it," Vampire Umpire said.

"What?" Jessica Aubrey asked.

"You know, sail the boat a bit."

"I'm sorry, I don't fully understand what you mean."

"Oh, right. I mean sail the ship."

"Yes, that wasn't quite my objection. However, your shaky grasp of naval terminology does make me wonder why you think you're qualified to command a vessel of over sixty thousand tonnes, carrying five thousand passengers, many of whom wish to survive the voyage?"

"I mean," Molly said. "I used to be really good at tying knots? And I know over three words for ship."

"So four words?"

"Ship. Boat. Yacht." Molly stopped. She had been enumerating each answer on her fingers, and now three stood proud in the air but began to waver like badly made skyscrapers in an earthquake. Finally she noticed Vampire Umpire mouthing a word at her and she said, "Wessel. I mean vessel," and raised her fourth finger in triumph.

"I don't think our insurance will cover it," Jessica Aubrey said, "and though Vampire Umpire is a good friend of mine, I doubt it will be possible."

"Got ya," Molly said, and winked.

"No, I mean it."

"Riiiiight," Molly said and winked again.

Seeing the likely turn of the conversation as clearly as she did that of the tides, Captain Aubrey spoke to Vampire Umpire instead. "Are you going to the costume party tonight?" she asked.

"Wouldn't miss it," he said. "I have brought costumes for both Molly and myself."

"As if my luggage wasn't heavy enough already," Molly muttered scowling.

"I look forward to seeing that," the captain said. "You're always so very inventive. It was one of my favourite things about dating you." She smiled shyly at Vampire Umpire and Molly found herself flushing. She turned to talk to Cecily Cholmondeley instead, and that woman was as friendly as her surname suggested so the dinner proceeded pleasurably.

◆

"Wow," said Molly, "This is a lot like why my brutally slain boyfriend wore incredibly oversized trousers – a *lot* of ballroom."

They stood atop a staircase with a solid mahogany bannister that in shape and sweep brought to mind the f hole of a violin. They looked out into a sea of chandeliers set in golden arcs and festooned with pendant crystals. The room was lucent. On the floor below them, people danced arrayed in costumes diverse and strange. Some wore clothes from past eras, which in quality seemed to be originals, others made a Wold Newton world of fictional characters, interacting with glee even with arch enemies – a Red Pokémon trainer and a Blue Pokémon trainer were even making out in the corner, even though their differences should have been insurmountable.

Captain Aubrey met them at the bottom of the stairs. "I might have known" she said, looking at Molly's costume.

"I had purchased a Wonder Woman costume for her," Vampire Umpire said. "And not a quick and unsatisfactory knock off, like wearing some shorts and a T-shirt with Wonder Woman's name on it. But I am afraid she insisted…"

Molly had, Vampire Umpire supposed shanghaied was the appropriate word, a passing sailor and insisted on borrowing his spare uniform for the party, fraudulently claiming she had no costume of her own. She had then used stationary to fashion a simple tricorn hat, and written the word captain on another piece of paper that she had glued to the jacket, with (it would turn out) impossible to remove super glue.

"I'm the captain!" Molly said and beamed with pride. "Couldn't you just see me, I don't know, like… standing behind the ship's wheel a bit, steering wildly and boldly?"

"In my nightmares perhaps," Captain Aubrey said. "And what are you meant to be, Vampire Umpire?"

"There's a leak on the boat!" Molly yelled extremely loudly in excitement. Many of the passengers stared around in panic and began stampeding towards the exits and the life boats. One woman was screaming in terror, and a man pushed her down and she began to be trodden under the feet of the fleeing crowd. Chaos rippled and spread through the ballroom like a virus infecting a swinger's colony.

"The ship is fine," Captain Aubrey roared, her voice simultaneously calm but Stentorian. "Everyone remain calm." Her authority, and the actions of her crewmen, calmed the crowd. "And what did you mean by that breathtakingly irresponsible act?" she hissed angrily at Molly.

"Jeez," Molly said. "He's dressed as a leek?" She gestured at Vampire Umpire, who was wearing very tight white trousers and a great spill of green fabrics designed to simulate the bland vegetable.

"To be fair to her, I am a leek," Vampire Umpire said.

Once the captain dismissed them, Molly having agreed to make up for what the captain perhaps unfairly characterised as "an attempted mutiny" by playing an exhibition tennis match the next day, they wandered around the room. The bottom part of Vampire Umpire's leek costume was too constricting to allow him to dance, but they gathered plates of food, both for Molly, and plenty of drink, which they shared, and mingled with the guests. Many had heard of her achievements on the tennis circuit and regarded her with interest; several more knew her as the "sinking hoax" girl, and viewed her less charitably.

On their second circuit of the room, they heard a man say, "For fuck's sake," loudly, and, their attention drawn, saw Ioana and Jeb Moslius standing nearby. Ioana was dressed in some kind of white shroud that she had covered in thousands, possibly tens of thousands, of cotton balls, and was wearing a gold foil crown. Moslius wore a pretty standard tuxedo.

"Good to see you both," Vampire Umpire said.

"It is always good to see you, Vampire Umpire," Ioana said, and touched his arm almost without noticing. Moslius grabbed her arm and pulled her to his side. "You are, what are you meant to be?"

"A leek," he said. "So it is like I'm a leek but since we are, to quote one of the twenty-first centuries better poets, on a boat, straight flowing on a boat on the deep blue sea, it's a pun on boats springing a leak."

"I do not understand," Ioana said. "Do leeks sometimes grow on boats? Because of the humidity?"

"I'll explain it later," Moslius spat, scowling.

'And what are you meant to be, Moslius?" Molly asked. "Or are you just pretending to be a tennis player, like every other day?"

"I'm James Bond," he said.

"An alcoholic, incompetent, misogynist?" Vampire Umpire asked.

"Seems right to me," Molly said. "What are you, Ioana?"

"Oh, Jeb asked me to come as a… what was the term? A classy hoar."

"So the cotton balls are the fog and the crown makes it classy?" Molly said as Moslius was saying, "I said I wanted you to be a fancy whore."

Vampire Umpire's polite smile vanished as completely as if it were his reflection and his face was a mirror. "You are an impolite man, Moslius, and I need not therefore be courteous to you. Ioana, perhaps I will see you some other day on the voyage. Good evening, only to you."

Molly said, "Yeah, laters, chummmmmm…ps," and followed her friend. Not long after, they ran into Cecily. The woman was wearing a black wig, with hair that hung just past her shoulders, and a dress with a décolletage so deep it was practically scraping the sea bed. Glued to her torso was a papier mâché structure of brown painted planks and pillars, with small coils of thread dyed with tea dotted around. Molly realised it was a dock.

"I'm Katy Pier-y," Cicely said.

They spent the rest of the night laughing and drinking with her.

♦

The captain knocked on Molly and Vampire Umpire's cabin door one hour before dawn. Her face was drawn, but it seemed more than tiredness had etched the worry lines in her brow and emptied the bags below her eyes. "Come with me," she said.

She led them to another state room, which she entered without knocking. There was a long trail of blood, leading out of the bathroom and along the floor to the side of the bed. They heard a beeping, from a hardwired phone that had not been replaced in its cradle.

"Go and look," Jessica Aubrey said.

They walked around the side of the bed. Cecily Cholmondeley lay on the floor, the blood smeared phone still in her hand, and a large wound gaping in her side. Her eyes were open, and stared lifeless at the ceiling.

Chapter Sixteen

"Where were you both at four am?" Captain Aubrey asked.

"Shouldn't the police be asking that?" Molly said. While she had never been in trouble with the law, she had seen a number of shows in which murders happen and the police investigate to try to determine who the murderer was as correctly as they possibly could.

"We're in the middle of the Atlantic Ocean," the captain said. "I am the only authority here. There is a retired detective on board, and I will consult him later, but my main aim is to keep panic to a minimum. Vampire Umpire," she continued. "I know you didn't do this, but you two were with Mrs. Cholmondeley almost the entire night. If word does spread, can you prove you're innocent?"

"Oh, I see how it is!" said Molly, indignant. "So you don't think I could drive a boat and now you also don't think I could commit a murder." She hesitated. "Actually, yeah, that's probably okay with me."

"Molly was asleep," Vampire Umpire said. "And I was simply reading. So we have no foolproof alibi, though I think most would accept it."

"Okay," the captain said. "Go back to your room."

◆

"She was our friend," Molly said.

"Yes." Vampire Umpire hesitated. "Over the centuries, I have lost many friends to death, some peacefully, others not. But it never becomes an easy thing." He hugged Molly, and she realised she was crying. He held her for a long time before she spoke again.

"What's going to happen?"

"I don't know," said Vampire Umpire. "Jessica is a good person, but she's not an investigator. And when we dock, the people leave the ship and I fear the chance of catching Cecily's killer will be gone just as fast as them."

"*We* have to figure it out," Molly said.

"We're not police officers," he protested.

"But we're smart. We can do this." She could sense him wavering. "We owe it to her," she said.

"Okay," he said. "I cannot promise we'll succeed, but we shall try."

"I bet it was Moslius anyway," she said. "That guy's a dick."

◆

The first task of the day, though, was not investigatory: the captain insisted on Molly undertaking the exhibition tennis match, citing the need to avoid any disruption to the ship's events and any concomitant disruption in the mood of the passengers. Molly managed to borrow some tennis equipment from the ship's stores and made her way to the top deck where the court was.

First she played the ship's pro, but he didn't make a particularly strong showing against her. In fact, after he lost the first sixteen points in a row, he hurled his racquet into the sea and began to sob into the net, which was not a traditional strategy for doing well in tennis. So Molly ended up lining the other side of the court with eight members of the watching crowd and playing against all of them. They still lost every point, but the shame was divided between them so it was more manageable.

Afterwards, having signed autographs for a few members of the crowd, she went back below decks. As she neared the threshold of the door, a large clang resounded behind her and she turned to see an anchor embedded in the deck. She looked up but saw no-one there, and simply informed the next crew member she passed. "An anchor?" he said.

"Yeah, like Popeye has tattooed on his arm." She hesitated. 'Except larger and made of metal instead of ink."

"Oh, I understand figurative language," the crew person said. "I'm a sailor and poetry runs through our veins like brine and blood."

"Cool."

"It must have come from the captain's anchor collection. She keeps a collection of classic anchors," the woman said.

"Well okay then," Molly said. She hadn't really wanted a long conversation about it, and the need to shower was becoming pressing, as the sweat from her back was about to meet the sweat from her butt and those two things are streams never meant to be crossed. "I'm going now, bye."

"Good bye, madam."

◆

When she came out of the bathroom, Vampire Umpire was sitting dressed on his unused bed, finishing a book of poetry. "Is it safe for you to be up?" Molly asked.

"I mean, a good amount of sleep is important, but I'm not at risk of dying from the lack of it," he replied.

"No, I mean the sun."

"Ah, yes." He shrugged. "I figured if we stay below decks, it should be fine. You will just have to close the curtains in any room we enter."

Of course the corridors, being internal, lacked any natural light, and they were able to travel to Cecily's room with no worries. The door was locked, but Molly knew a few tricks with hairpins, which made her lovely hair easier to control and fix into attractive shapes and styles. And now she removed two of those hairpins and used them to pick the lock, which she also knew how to do.

The body had been removed, but the rest of the room was unchanged. There was still the trail of blood from the bathroom to the spot where she had finally died, and the phone had yet to be either cleaned or replaced. Vampire Umpire knelt and sniffed the exsanguinated fluid.

"You getting hungry, Vampire Nompire?" Molly asked.

"No: I like my blood like Chris Hemsworth likes his penis: inside someone else's body."

"So what you doing? You checking they vacuum often enough? Because I had a friend who worked at a hotel chain whose name I can't tell you but it rhymes with Frump, and he said usually they just picked carpets the same colour as shed human skin and used the money saved on cleaners to go down the dogfights at Christmas. He said the boss of the chain would usually get in the ring and try to fight the dogs himself. The smaller dogs anyway: anything below a poodle and it was POW, right in the dog-kisser."

"The blood smells wrong," Vampire Umpire said. "I can tell with my vampire scent powers."

"She might have been on medication for something? She was a lively old gal but she was also old. I mean lively, too. But old as old balls."

"Maybe," said Vampire Umpire. "It's hard to tell from this." They looked through the bathroom cabinets, but other than some Rogaine that presumably belonged to George St. Drake and some Veet that Molly fervently hoped belonged to Cecily, there was nothing even remotely medical. Cecily did use a fancy toothpaste, though, which Molly swiped as her own was running low.

In the state room they searched and found nothing of interest. Specifically, the nothing that was of interest was the room's safe, which was open and empty. Molly said, "Do you think she was robbed?"

"It's hard to say. The captain may have cleared out the safe just to be…"

"You're trying to think of a word other than safe there, aren't you?"

"… Careful!" Vampire Umpire shouted triumphantly. More calmly, he repeated, "Jessica may have cleared out the safe just to be careful."

"Well played," Molly said.

"I think we need to call her down to our cabin," Vampire Umpire said.

"Finally giving me that hree-way I am always asking for?"

"Well maybe, but I meant more to ask about the case."

"Yeah… Maybe see if we can get a go on that ship's wheel, too."

♦

The captain came down to the cabin readily enough, a testament either to her friendship with Vampire Umpire or her not hearing Molly prattling on about three-ways and ship's wheels when he made the call. She brought with her a man with jet black hair marred by a streak of white that ran forward over its natural parting and made a kiss curl like a bow-wave over his forehead. He had a luxuriant moustache that initially looked as if he had for some reason glued a top rat to his upper lip. Vampire Umpire had known familiars who had done that to more readily have access to blood, but in this case the fur addendum proved to be an actual moustache. His voice was plummy and booming, like someone had put a bomb in a fruit basket.

"Now you listen to me, you pair of Scotch cousins," he bellowed. "I'm the investigator here, and it's my balls on the line."

"Scotch cousins?" Vampire Umpire asked while Molly wondered what kind of line the man had put his balls on. "Is it like a fishing line?" she asked. "Balls can get dangly when men get older," she confided to the room at large. "He probably wants to keep them from tumbling out the bottom of his trousers."

"Scotch cousins is an expression for idiots we use in Engleland," he said, with odd pronunciation. "Because the scotch are often as thick as the mists that choke their cities, which obscuring fog is why they both eat bizarre almost meats and accidentally mate with their siblings. And my balls are high and tight as an alcoholic acrobat, thanking you for your concern. It is purely a metaphorical line on which I have placed the boys, who are named Holmes and Watson, if you must know, because one is long and thin and the other one is squat and portly."

Both Vampire Umpire and Molly said nothing, as their questions had been answered both completely and graphically. Captain Jessica said, "Inspector Elliot has arrested George St. Drakes," she said.

"We found his straight razor buried in the woman's guts," Elliot said, "and he obviously fled the cabin after the attack, leaving her to die."

"So the case is closed," Jessica said. "And while I appreciate you liked the woman, you shouldn't get involved, Vampire Umpire."

"What about the safe?" Vampire Umpire asked. "Did you empty that?"

"No," she said. "But it was empty when I got there."

"St. Drake must have opened it," Elliott said. "He's concealed the loot somewhere, either on the ship or up his anus, and either way it's got to come out eventually."

"Would you mind if we spoke to him?" Molly asked. "He had a recipe for lobster bisque that he promised me and my gut's achin' for some crustacean." A sensitive reader would note the clever rhyme in that line of dialogue.

Vampire Umpire looked at Jessica, who sensed that Molly was perhaps being a little deceptive, with imploration and some hint of vampire hypnotic power in his eyes, and Jessica sighed. "Fine. The inspector will take you to see him."

"I'm not a babysitter," Inspector Elliot said, "and I'm meeting a lively widow for some intercourse in the bar, and then hopefully a different kind of intercourse in her bedroom. I don't like using mine, because why should I have to clean the sheets when she's the one getting my seed?"

"Fine," said Jessica. "I'll call down to the brig and tell them you're coming, as long as the Inspector tells us no more about his romantic endeavours."

◆

George St. Drake was locked into a small cell in the lowest quarters of the ship. Small, at least, in comparison to the rest of the rooms: it was still larger than the average person's bedroom. He sat on the edge of a cot, dressed no longer in a suit but instead in simple white cotton bottoms and shirt. His shoes were still his own, but the laces were removed.

"I say, you couldn't ask for my laces back, could you?" was his first comment on seeing them. "I can't bear to be in here another second."

"Suicide is too easy an out for you," Molly said angrily.

"Suicide? Gosh, no," said St. Drake. "I just want to make cat's cradles with them. I'm frightfully bored."

"Did you kill Cecily?" Vampire Umpire asked.

"Of course not!"

"So why weren't you in the room? Why was she alone?" Molly said. Her eyes were as Fury-filled as someone looking really close-up at a picture of Samuel L. Jackson.

"Cecily said I was too boring and she kicked me out," he said. "I was trying to find somewhere to sleep, but all I could find was a lifeboat on deck. They found me there, wrapped in a tarp." He crossed his arms and placed his palms in his armpits, and lifted his feet off the floor.

"Cold are you?" Molly asked.

"Incredibly. Not been this cold since I was a child in the slums of…" he stopped, but just a bit too late.

"The slums of where? Aren't you meant to be some kind of posh twat who wouldn't know what those words would mean?" Molly said, jabbing her finger hard into his chest. "Like a slum to you should be a house with only twelve dining rooms."

"Look, alright. My name's not George St. Drake, okay?" He glanced around them at the door to see if anyone was listening and said, "It's Jorge Drag-on."

"Jorge Dragon?"

"No, Drag-on, like my conversation was wont to do, my ma always said."

"So you're saying…?"

"I was born an impoverished child in the slums of Rio de Janeiro," he said, his voice admittedly droning like a Godspeed You! Black Emperor song. "To a large family, of poor and lowly origin, with no great antecedents to bring pride to our lineage. By day we wandered the favela trying to pick pocket tourists. By night we shared our takings and huddled for warmth, if we were lucky around the corpse of a found deceased canine that we burned and on which we cooked any viands our impecunious state could grant us."

"I guess he's speaking a lot of Portugese words, right?" Molly asked Vampire Umpire.

"No, it's English. Just as inflated and pompous as him."

"May I continue?" They nodded. "One day a rich man grabbed my hand as it reached into his pocket. He interrogated me on my situation, and took me – having consulted with my mother, I wasn't McCanned – to stay at his villa."

"Oh boy," said Molly. "This is going to get really dark, isn't it?"

"Everyone I have ever loved has died," Vampire Umpire said, "and even I fear what's coming next."

"He had a room in his house where at first I was forbidden entry," Drag-on dragged on. "And many nights was I there awake in my bower wondering what dwelled within. One night I gained entry by means of impropriety."

"Broke in," Vampire Umpire said to Molly, who had looked at him quizzically.

"Inside were DVDs of every costume drama the BBC had ever done! For nights, I watched them and learned how rich men of character were meant to behave. But then my host found me and, fearing my additional usage would scratch his precious DVDs, he cast me back into the streets."

"To be fair, the man was right," Molly said. "DVDs aren't cheap and you were going to ruin them."

"But I knew now how life was to be lived. It was meant to be handsome men and women banqueting on finely cooked dishes at tables laid with sterling silver and thick linen. Not ripping meat shreds out of some fresh-ish roadkill's eye lining."

"I think, maybe, there might be a middle ground?" Molly pondered.

"I discovered too, that when I speak people are often so bored they stop paying attention to me. So I sneaked back into the rich man's house and stole some money for clothes, and then began conning my way around the world. The wealthy never noticed my lies, because I was too boring to pay attention to. Because the things I said were of so little interest, I never got caught out."

"You said that three times," Vampire Umpire said.

"Oh. Sorry. I assumed you weren't paying attention. People often don't when I talk."

"Jeez, we get it," Molly cussed.

"What was in the safe?" Vampire Umpire asked Drag-on.

"I don't know, Cecily never showed me," he said. "I'm sure the captain might be able to effect its opening?"

"Give us a minute, Drag-on," Molly said. "What do you think?" she asked Vampire Umpire.

"I don't think he did it," Vampire Umpire said. "If he wanted to kill someone, he'd bore them to death, not stab them." He turned back to Drag-on. "Did Cecily have any other friends on the ship?"

"Other than you two, there were three: Misthalia Hengis, Gusticia Wind and Augustinia Thrush. They often travelled together." He wrote down their suite numbers on a piece of paper Vampire Umpire handed him.

"Okay," said Molly. "Could you tell us their names and room numbers please?" She turned to Vampire Umpire and said, "We both know where we're going next."

Chapter Seventeen

Vampire Umpire sat and watched as Molly thoroughly interrogated the buffet. She had his plate, covered in a wide selection of noodles, and her own, filled with curries of various different spice combinations and more kinds of meat than a particularly politically correct male strip club. She placed them in front of her on the table and demonstrated a startling ambidexterity in shovelling food from both into her mouth. In almost no time, the food was finished and it only took three more pairs of plates to stuff her fuller than a foie gras goose.

"Can we go investigate the murder now?" he asked. "Or do you want pudding?"

"Pud-ding*s*," she corrected.

A short time after that, they were ready to commence what both hoped would be the final stages of the investigation. Vampire Umpire because he wanted to find the killer of his friend; Molly for the same reason but also because dinner would be starting in four hours.

♦

Misthalia Hengis had hair a shade of red that had never before occurred in nature and a face that had been lifted so many times that when her lips parted her forehead squeaked. She wore a black Chanel dress and a gold chain so fine a bacterium could have flossed with it. She met them in the living room of her stateroom, where she offered them petits four of fine sculpted fondant and delicate, almost wispy sponge, and coffee. Her bedroom door was open, and through it they could see the taut, muscular buttocks of a nude man who, judging by the greatness of his gluteus, was perhaps forty years her junior. She followed Vampire Umpire's stare and said, "Quite tired him out, I'm afraid."

"Too much bingo?" Molly asked.

"Something like that," Misthalia said. She winked at Vampire Umpire. "I like your friend: she's so young and innocent."

"Hey, I know what was going on really!" Molly said.. She smiled knowingly. "You were playing bingo… for money."

"How did you know Cecily?" Vampire Umpire asked, deciding to take control of the conversation before it could spiral out of hand, like a novelist who expertly shapes reality instead of just an exquisitely judged book.

"Oh CC? She and I have known each other for too long to remember."

"Still, could you try?"

Misthalia contorted her face until her forehead almost frowned. "I'm not sure. I think her second husband was my third husband? Or... No, I married one of her lovers for a few months when we were in Amalfi, I think. Haha, that's right: I took him back to Britain with me and then just abandoned him, and CC had a devil of a time getting him back home. One of my best pranks."

"Did she have any enemies?" Molly asked.

"Well Nelson Mandela has always been a bit jealous of how much money she gave to charity, but I think that's more a friendly rivalry than a serious animosity." Misthalia turned her head like a dog that thought it had been offered a car ride but was uncertain if said car ride might end at the vet's. "Did you use the past tense?"

"Well yes? You can't have enemies once you're dead, unless you're a vampire," Molly said. Then she panicked and added, "And of course those definitely don't exist hahahahahahaha." She looked at both her co-conversationalists and, judging that she hadn't seemed casual enough, continued for about another quarter of a minute, "Hahahahaha."

"Cecily is dead?" Misthalia asked, clearly shocked. A clear fluid began leaking from her eyebrows and trickling down over her eyelids to splat on her cheeks with a sound like fingers drumming on a tom-tom. The liquid caused her eye-shadow and mascara to leak, turning her face into a Salvador Dali illustration of a face.

"I'm so sorry, I assumed you knew," Vampire Umpire said. 'Especially as we told you on the phone we were coming to talk about her murder."

"I thought you meant there was trouble with her crows back home and she wanted to borrow my aviarist to sort them again," Misthalia sobbed. She plucked tissues from a dispenser and dabbed at her eyebrows.

"Why is that happening?" Molly asked, in horror, fascination, and horrified fascination.

"My doctor had to move my tear ducts after the last surgery."

"It looks completely normal," Vampire Umpire said solicitously. "He does good work."

"Thank you-hoo-hoo," said Misthalia, the words turning into another fit of bawling.

"Let's go," Molly said. "We're not going to get more information out of her, and no-one would fake a grief that looked like... that," she said, gesturing at Misthalia's whole situation.

◆

"Gusticia Wind?" Vampire Umpire asked.

"Please," she said. "Call me Gusty." Gusty was only a few years older than Molly and though vastly less beautiful was dressed much more fancily, making the latter feel a little hoboish. Gusty was wearing a pale blue Givenchy dress and a matching sun hat, with silver Sophia Webster sandals. By contrast, Molly was wearing a pair of jeans, a T-shirt that read "Tennis Players

Have The Freshest Balls" and was barefoot because she had not been able to find her shoes that morning.

Vampire Umpire had, in fact, placed them outside the room for cleaning, but the ship staff had assumed the tattered and ragged foot holsters had been placed there to be destroyed. He did intend, when night fell, to go to one of the deck shops and try to buy her replacements but, while few would call him a coward, he didn't want to tell her what had happened until he had replaced them.

Gusty's rooms were adjacent to Misthalia's, and exactly as nice. "Pretty sweet suite," Molly said.

"Thank you. My husband only buys the best for me." Gusty smiled. "Which is of course why he has me."

"What does he do?" Vampire Umpire asks.

"Mostly just he likes to watch," she said.

"Uhhh…" said Vampire Umpire, while Molly added, "You mean he likes the movies a lot?"

"Oh, you meant for a job? Let me check." She took out her iPhone and typed for a few moments, then inspected the results. "He manufactures the briefcases that rich people use to carry around their bribe money, according to Wikipedia."

"Well, I suppose the briefcases could be used for other things too," Vampire Umpire said.

"No," said Gusticia. "Only for bribe money."

"Yeah," said Molly. "As Marcus Aurelius tells us, of each thing ask, what itself is it? What is its nature?"

"I've always felt," Gusty said, "that when we construct physical objects it is entirely an attempt to ensnare the noumenon, the thing that exists beyond and without all physical perceptions."

"Cant about Kant?" Molly said. "I can't. At least, this early in the day and this sober."

"I am sorry to tell you," Vampire Umpire said, "especially as it interrupts this fascinating philosophical colloquy, that Cecily Cholmondeley is dead."

"Oh, I heard," Gusty said.

"You don't seem sad about it?" Molly said.

"It's the last challenge, isn't it?" Gusty said. "That moment, Heidegger tells us, we spend all our life preparing for – the ascent to complete selfhood that death allows us."

"You don't instead follow Jaspers view? That death grants us transcendence into some ultimate, illusion-devoid form of reality?" Molly asked.

"A fine idea, if it weren't completely unverifiable and thus nonsense," Gusty said.

"Well," said Molly raising an eyebrow, "I guess de Gusty-bus non est disputandum."

"I like you," Gusty said.

"But did you like Cecily?" Vampire Umpire asked, seguing as neatly as any San Francisco tech-start-up millionaire.

"Of course I did," she said. "She and I used to game the casinos together, all along Les Spélugues in Monte Carlo." She shook her head. She had strawberry blonde hair and the great sheaf of it shook like a theatre curtain behind which someone was pretending to be a ghost. "I'm never going to find anyone who steals bust cards as neatly at blackjack as her."

"I'm super good at cards," Molly said. "In fact I have never once lost a game of snap. And I bet I could learn this 'black jack' really quickly."

Gusty stared at Molly's outfit and said, "Well, next time we're both in Monaco, I suppose we can give it a go?"

◆

Outside the cabin, Vampire Umpire asked, "Did you really have to insist on her making you coffee just so you could throw it at her?"

"I feel I made the right choice."

"She *was* rude to you, I suppose," said Vampire Umpire. "And you do clean up real nice, unlike her dress or her couch."

"Heheheh," Molly sniggered, remembering it fondly. "Plus if she is the murderer, she'll now probably try to kill me. So really it was all a clever ruse on my part, which you failed to see, idiot."

They began walking to the last interview they had, the room being a few decks down. As they would pass their own room on the way, Molly decided to stop in. "I want to clean my teeth before dinner," she said. "They feel grotty after lunch and all those cakes Misthalia gave me."

"Sure," said Vampire Umpire.

"And maybe you can have another look for my shoes?"

"But of course I will," he said. "It is odd I cannot find them with my vampire senses, but I sure hope they haven't been stolen or accidentally destroyed even though a friend will replace them in that case or anything."

Vampire Umpire was lying on one of the beds reading when Molly stepped out of the bathroom. "Are my shoes in that book?" she asked. She was holding her toothbrush with a small blob of toothpaste sitting on it.

"I already checked the room using my vampire speed," he protested, falsely.

"Hmmm," said Molly. She raised the toothbrush to her mouth. Vampire Umpire was immediately beside her, grabbing the toothbrush before the white fluid could pass her lips, like brushus interruptus. He smelled it.

"That's the same smell I detected in Cecily's room," he said. "But stronger. This toothpaste has been poisoned."

"Then I guess brushing twice a day would keep the dentist away," Molly said. "Because they don't usually see dead people."

"The murderer must have known we were investigating and somehow poisoned our toothpaste too," Vampire Umpire said.

"Oh, no," corrected Molly. "This is Cecily's toothpaste. I stole it because mine was running low and because it's really nice."

"I guess that is a good reason to interfere with a crime scene," he said.

"Hey, we're a tennis player and an umpire wandering around trying to solve a murder the authorities already believe to be solved. We don't have to be super professional."

"Fine, fine. I'll sneak the toothpaste back into her room later and we can tell the detective about it."

"But who poisoned it? Will there be fingerprints?"

"You mean other than yours?"

"Fair point. I'll wipe this down and we'll solve the murder some other way."

Right then there was a knock on the door, and they let Inspector Elliot into the room. "I've had a number of messages from Captain Aubrey," he said. "About you two upsetting a guest, stealing a whole bunch of her cakes, hurling coffee at another passenger and just generally running hogwild like two buffoons."

"Inspector," said Molly. "We believe we have discovered Cecily Cholmondeley was poisoned. If you check her room, you will find a toothpaste tube there that will make not just your teeth but your entire body go white."

"I don't get it," the inspector said.

"Because, y'know, dead people are pale? And toothpaste is meant to make your teeth white?"

"I got it and liked it," Vampire Umpire said.

"Thank you," she said. She hugged him, taking the chance to plant the toothpaste tube into his pocket. "Go," she whispered.

"Also, Inspector, do you not think *this* has some bearing on the investigation?" She gestured flamboyantly around their room.

"What?" he said.

"This," she said, if anything enlarging the gesture.

"What am I meant to be seeing?" She gestured again. "Why won't you just say what it is?" She waved. "Is it that painting you mean?"

In the interim, Vampire Umpire had used his vampire speed and vampire stealthiness to return the poisoned toothpaste.

"No," the inspector said. "As far as I can tell, this painting of a sunset is entirely unrelated to the murder."

"Well," said Molly, "then I guess just check out that toothpaste thing. I can't be right all the time: even a working clock gets broken twice a day."

♦

Augustinia Thrush's room was far less grand than the other two women's. She let them in and sat on the edge of the single bed. Molly sat in the chair on the far side of the bed opposite the door, and Vampire Umpire stood awkwardly in the corner of the room. There was no porthole, and the room was lit by a stark bare bulb.

"How can I help you?" she said.

"We're investigating Cecily's murder," Molly said.

"Oh, I see," Thrush said.

"How did you know her."

"I'm her accountant."

"That must be int…" Molly tried to say.

"As a profession that is fasc…" Vampire Umpire managed before his innate honesty also stopped him. They sat quietly for about a minute, struggling for anything to say.

"Yes, fine," Thrush said. She was looking at her lap to avoid eye contact with them, and she swept one hand through her bobbed hair. A glimmer of green sparkled in the room light.

"Oh my god," Molly said. "You're the murderer."

"What?" said Augustinia, and her pasty skin flushed.

"Those are Cecily's earrings!" Molly pointed.

"She loaned them to me," Thrush said.

Vampire Umpire could smell Cecily's scent on the air, and he opened the bedside drawer, where he found a pile of cash and several large money orders. "And these too?" he asked.

Augustinia Thrush glared at them both, then yelled, 'This bird's gonna fly!" and standing, hurled the bed over and at them, and sprinted out the door.

Vampire Umpire caught the bed in one hand and rested it against the wall. "Come on," Molly said.

They were in the corridor chasing after Thrush in moments, and saw her slam open a door onto the open deck ahead of them. Sunlight waited heavy and bright outside. They stopped. "I can't get her," Vampire Umpire said.

"I'll do it," Molly said.

"Are you sure?"

"Yes," said Molly. "I even have these handcuffs I swiped from the inspector while you were out of the room. So I'm all prepared for when I catch her."

"I mean hopefully you will do," he said. "She's getting an increasingly unfair head start."

"It'll be fine," Molly said. "You might not think it to look at me, but I can run like the wind blows." She turned and began to run, then came back. "I didn't steal the handcuffs for sex reasons," she said implausibly. "It was in case I needed to make a citizen's arrest."

♦

Molly burst on the deck and followed the woman's path in the disorder she had caused. She had turned upstairs, judging by the man sprawled at the base of the steps, and Molly raced upwards after her. On the very top deck, she saw Thrush running for the bridge. She was limping, clearly cramping, and Molly, whose legs were pumping clean and fast, was sure she would catch her soon.

A pile of young men sprawled into her path, and she shouted, "Out of my way, I have to catch Thrush."

This incited a chorus of replies, including "Not many people look for that," and one smarmy man who said, "If you're looking to get Thrush, you can spend half an hour in my room," and grabbed her arm. It was Moslius. When he realised who he had hit on, he cursed and said, "Oh, it's you."

"God, you're gross," Molly said, and knocked him down. She ran again after Thrush, who had now entered the bridge.

There were two doorways, and Molly ran to the far one, reasoning that Thrush would probably bolt the nearer one first. She was right: that was exactly what the woman was doing when Molly kicked in the far door. Captain Aubrey was lying on the floor, and from the blood seeping out of her forehead, Molly suspected she was not just taking a work nap.

"Stay back," Thrush said. She was holding a flare gun and pointed it at Molly's heart.

"What's your plan, here?" Molly asked her. "A cruise liner is not exactly a getaway vessel."

Right then, Moslius appeared behind her. "You can't just knock me down," he began, before noticing the situation.

"Help me," Thrush said to Moslius. "She murdered Cecily and I found out and now she's trying to kill me."

The woman's story was transparently ridiculous but Molly could see Moslius thinking, and wondered if he saw now a way to beat her in a way he never seemed able to on a tennis court. She felt his hands close around her upper arms and adrenaline sharpened her perception so that she could see the skin at the joint of Augustinia's knuckle whiten as her hand tensed on the trigger of the gun.

A nun burst into the room, knocking Moslius to the side and pouncing on Augustinia Thrush. The figure slammed Thrush's head against the deck and the woman's fingers relaxed, the gun falling from them. Molly realised that the nun was actually Vampire Umpire wrapped in several dark quilts and quickly clipped Moslius hard on the jaw.

"You okay?" Vampire Umpire asked. He rested against the ship's control panel, and she saw his skin was steaming slightly.

"Pretty much," Molly said. "Thank you."

"Happy to do it," he said. "Shall we try to wake Captain Aubrey?"

"In a minute," she said, moving towards him. "There's something I want to do first."

◆

"I can't thank you enough," Aubrey said when they had explained everything. Augustinia Thrush still lay unconscious at their feet but the inspector was on his way to accompany her first to the medical room for tests and then to the brig. "Finding the true culprit may have saved my career. I wouldn't like to think the kind of resources a man like St. Drake might possess to use against someone who falsely accused him of murder."

"Less than you might think," Molly said, but quietly.

"Plus it wouldn't have been fun trying to listen to him in court," Aubrey added.

"It has all worked out quite smoothly," Vampire Umpire said.

"Except what about this man?" Aubrey gestured at Moslius, who was handcuffed to the ship's wheel. "Was he in it with her?"

"Oh… um, no," said Molly. "He just followed me in when I came to stop Thrush. But, uh… he got all excited and started trying to steer the ship, and since I know how you feel about how it should only be the freshest, best seamen getting on that wheel," at which phrasing Vampire Umpire still smirked, despite being vastly more mature than even the most aged wines and cheeses, "I thought I had better stop him pretty fast.

So I gave him a little of the old chin music," she finished, miming punching the air. She then gilded the lilt a bit by adding, "And that might be why the ship is a few miles of course. It took us about an hour to bring you around."

Aubrey looked at Molly sceptically. Her hands certainly did seem slightly brown-tinged, in the same shade as the oil Aubrey used to keep the wood of the wheel from cracking.

Vampire Umpire said, "I was here the whole time, and that is exactly what happened." He looked long at Aubrey.

The murderer had been caught, the ship was safe and, checking the GPS, not too far off course. Aubrey supposed she could let it go.

"Fine," she said. "Obviously Mr. Moslius will have to spend the rest of the trip in the brig, for hijacking the ship. But we're only three days from New York, I'm sure he'll survive."

"Thank you," Vampire Umpire said. "And in return I can promise you that nothing will be getting into this bridge except seamen from now until we dock."

◆

Vampire Umpire and Molly stood looking over the side of the ship. "We did it," he said, finally.

"Yes," said Molly. "I did it."

"I mean, I feel I helped a bit."

"How did you help? I did all the steering myself. You refused to even touch the wheel, saying 'it is a crime'."

"I see. I meant solved the murder. But you meant you had a go on the ship's wheel."

"Damn right I did," said Molly. "Now let's go, and you can replace those shoes of mine you threw out." A spray of sea air dusted across the railing and sprayed them. She spat. "Ugh. I'm all salty like seamen now."

Chapter Eighteen

Molly stepped towards the hotel room window and threw the curtains wide. "Welcome to New York," Molly said. "It's been waiting for you." Their room was high up and overlooked Central Park, which sprawled green and verdant and out of place in the forest of tall buildings and street noise and teeming human life. The sky was clear and New York under soft summer sunlight always looks like it's being shot in a movie.

Unfortunately, any sun was fatal to Vampire Umpire, so when Molly had opened the curtain he had leapt as rapidly as he could into the bathroom and closed over the door. "Vampire, remember?" he said.

"Oh Chumpire Umpire, are you worried about that?" Molly said. "I saw in a movie yesterday morning, you guys don't die, you just kind of sparkle and have romantic adventures." Nonetheless she closed the curtains again.

"Have you been watching Twilight?" he asked, incredulous. She opened the bathroom door and stepped in.

"No. I don't remember the name of it, but there were other monsters too, and the vampire fought them."

"Yeah, those were werewolves. You're talking about Twilight."

"Noo-ohh. They were weird scowling things that could unhinge their jaw and roared a lot."

"Yeah!" said Vampire Umpire. "Werewolves!" He raised his eyebrows on both words, for emphasis, and for good measure spread his arms.

"Hold on," Molly said, unlocking her phone, "let me check." She read for a bit, swiped around and then said, "See!" holding her phone triumphantly in his face, albeit too close to read. "It was called Blade II."

"Oh, right. But I'm not a day-walker."

"So I just…"

"Nearly killed me, yeah." He patted her arm consolingly. "But don't worry, it was an accident."

"I'm so sorry," she said. "I can't imagine what it would be like if…"

"It's okay," Vampire Umpire said. "Just shake it off. I'm fine." She hugged him to her, and he let her hold him until they were interrupted by a knock on the door. When they answered, the woman standing there had on a short black wig covered by a black polka-dotted headscarf and wore a pair of cat-eye Dolce and Gabbana sunglasses and lipstick so red it was like the colour of passion or obsession.

"Hi," she said.

"Hi," said Vampire Umpire. Both spoke flatly, their voices weighed down with some heavy freight of supressed emotion.

"Hey," Molly said brightly. "Are you here about room service, because I *would* like room service."

"Do you remember me?" the woman asked. "Standing in my nice dress, staring at the sunset, saying I would see you again someday?"

"And I told you you would, even if only in your wildest dreams," Vampire Umpire said.

"Do you know the room service girl, Vampire Chum-pire?" Molly made it clear with her flawless elocution that this time she was referencing the word chum, not chump. "You know so many people."

"I should never have left you there," the woman said. "But this is me standing in front of you, swallowing my pride, saying I'm sorry for that night."

"Come in," he said to the woman. "I'm sure we can order some actual room service, unless you've vastly changed career and you actually are here to take Molly's order."

◆

Vampire Umpire called for coffee and some cakes, and the woman sat down in one of the room's two couches. A low table separated them, and Vampire Umpire and Molly sat on the other side. The woman took off her glasses. "Molly, this is Taylor. Taylor, this is my good friend Molly."

"I'm sorry yehbuhwha?" Molly said.

"What do you mean?" Vampire Umpire asked.

"Is she epileptic?" Taylor asked. "I always try to keep strobe light effects to a minimum at my concerts because so many of my fans are epileptic."

"No, she's not epileptic," Vampire Umpire said. "I have no clue what's happening. It might be another curse." He explained about the attack on their lives in Rome.

Molly was now emitting a high-pitched sound, like an old-fashioned whistling kettle that had been left on the stove until almost all the water was gone and it was about to explode. She reached forward with her arms, like a sinner grasping futilely for salvation. Her mouth was twisted halfway between a smile and a sob, and her eyes were scrunched deep into her face, though not so tightly that tears were not shooting out like bursts from a super soaker. She toppled forward, and Vampire Umpire caught her before she could smash through the glass table.

When she woke, she was lying on the bed. "Are you okay?" Vampire Umpire asked. "You fainted."

"I didn't wee myself, did I?" Molly asked.

"No," said Vampire Umpire. "Not even on the bed."

"Ugh," said Taylor. "Katy Perry apparently passes out and does wees on hotel beds all the time. Wees being the *best case* scenario. It's why even though she's allegedly singer, in the hotel trade she's better known for the things that she does on the mattress. Ask anyone. One hundred percent true."

"You're Taylor Swift," Molly said. She said something else, which might have been "I love you more than anyone I have ever met or ever will," but she was too breathless for it to be audible.

"That's right," Taylor said, slowly and deliberately. She turned to Vampire Umpire and said, more quietly and faster, "Is she a bit...?"

"What do you mean?" he said.

"I forget the polite term," she said. "Is she a bit, y'know... *Kanye?*"

"Ohhhh," said Vampire Umpire as her meaning dawned. "No, I think she's just a fan. She sometimes sings your songs in her sleep, though with a bit less skill than you do."

"She's an angel," Molly whispered. A little louder, she said, "How on earth do you know Taylor Swift, Vampire Umpire?"

"Oh, that's easy," Taylor said. "A few years back, I was touring England and I took a break day to visit Sherwood forest. My car broke down and I had to camp for the night."

"I hate anything that inconveniences you, Taylor," Molly said. "And when I get back to England I will hunt down and kill that car."

"That's... nice," she said. "But there's no need. I had it repaired."

Vampire Umpire took up the story. "I was also travelling the country, visiting various acquaintances of mine. I visit England so rarely that I like to see as many of them as I can, as there may not be another trip for... quite some time."

"I'd built a fire outside," Taylor said. While Molly interjected, "You're so talented, Taylor," Taylor ignored her and continued. "I was sitting roasting smores on it when all of a sudden something heavy crashed into the flames and then, wow. Sparks fly."

"I heard someone screaming and ran to see if they were okay," Vampire Umpire said.

"I heard these sounds from all around me, so I got into my tent. And suddenly these things were clawing at the fabric."

"What were they?" Molly asked. "Oversize Lady Gaga fans?"

"No," said Taylor. "They were ents."

"So the Monsters turned out to be just trees?" Molly asked.

"Well kind of," Taylor said. "They were enraged as I had accidentally burnt a few twigs that belonged to one of the Ents."

"I believe it was his foot," Vampire Umpire said. "It grew back after a few years."

"Anyway, Vampire Umpire here speaks Entish and he explained everything and got them to let me live." Taylor smiled at him. "And after that we got... talking, and we dated for a while."

"Until the Kalahari Desert," he said. "When you wanted to go the lion sanctuary and they were only open during the day, even though you know they would have stayed open for you, and so you left me. And all I wished was that I knew how to be something you could miss."

"Vampire Umpire, you know you can only properly Lion King a lion cub in the rising sun," she said. "And I am sorry."

"It's fine," he said. "It's a long time ago now, and I always knew you were trouble." He smiled, and she smiled back at him like they shared a secret. "So how can I help you now? I'll help however I can, with the proviso that we are never getting back together. And I mean ever."

"I know that's not an option now," Taylor Swift said, and for a moment she looked as profoundly sad as Molly felt she had ever seen anyone. Taylor Swift was better even at experiencing emotions than anyone else. "I know people like you are gone forever when they say goodbye."

"Okay, so what do you need?"

"I've been experiencing… threats, lately," she said. "I don't even know what to call it. Strange things just keep happening around me. Like all the food in my pantry just suddenly, like, wilted. And members of my entourage keep getting sick and having to leave the tour. I see horrible sights in the corner of my eye, and I hear eerie music that almost captivates me."

"That's just your muse," Molly said. "You hear songs of beauty untellable by anyone but you. It is your gift to the world!"

"They aren't my songs," she said. "I don't know," she sighed. "My luck may just be bad, lately. I had my breakups, and nothing seems to go right for me. Maybe this is just that, but with you in town I just would feel better if you'd take a look around for me?"

"I guess we can," Vampire Umpire said. "But what about Drake? If the Dragon King of Mhendweun cannot protect you, I don't know what I can do."

"He has had to return to his people," Taylor said. "The dragon-kind are under attack from the Goat Lords." She half-smiled. "I guess I always find it impossible to keep a man for long."

"Ah, I didn't know things had got so serious so fast."

'We'll do anything to help you, Taylor," Molly yelled. "Do you need a cool back up dancer?" She started cavorting about the bedroom, throwing shapes (and furniture) around with, well, enthusiasm let's say.

"I have a concert tonight," she said. "I'll put you and your friend on the guest list, okay?" She tapped Molly on the shoulder, stilling the tennis genius' mad gyrations. "It was enchanting to meet you, Molly," she said.

◆

After the concert, Molly and Vampire Umpire went back stage. "That was amazing," Molly said. "All the songs were so good and I loved all of it."

"It was really good," Vampire Umpire said. "I have attended many concerts in my long descent through the centuries, and all of the great ones leave me feeling younger and invigorated. Tonight, I don't know about you, but I feel almost a youth again."

"Like you're twenty-two?"

"I guess," he said.

"Oh for fuck's sake," Molly said.

"What?"

"Look," she said and pointed, where they saw Jebediah Moslius and Ioana Dumitrescu standing at the craft service table back stage.

"Ah," said Vampire Umpire. "Well, I guess if we go over now, he'll probably get so annoyed at you he leaves?"

"Maybe, I guess. I don't know why he finds me so aggravating."

"It's a mystery to me as well," Vampire Umpire said. They walked over and said their hellos. For Vampire Umpire this consisted of greeting Ioana warmly and curtly saying Moslius' surname. Molly shook hands with Ioana and gave a perfunctory wave to Moslius, who just shrugged in response. Unfortunately, this dislodged a small piece of chicken from his plate, which collided with Molly's shoe. It was a breach of etiquette that any textbook on the subject would agree had three correct responses. Options 1 and 2 would be ignoring it and asking for an apology respectively.

Molly went with, "Someday I'll be big enough that you can't hit me, Moslius."

"What are you talking about?" he protested. "Last time we met, you knocked me out and handcuffed me to a ship's wheel and I spent four fucking days in prison."

"Well it's less time than you deserve!" Molly yelled. "You should have to be in jail for a thousand years for making people look at your horrible face!"

"I'll kill you," Moslius shouted and swung at Molly. The backstage security however had been attracted to the commotion and Molly simply let them grab his arm before the punch could land. They led him outside the theatre.

"Hopefully he's getting the roughing up he deserves," Molly said, looking around at her friend and Moslius' girlfriend. However, in doing so she noticed Taylor was free and immediately dashed over to speak to her.

Vampire Umpire watched her go and smiled with pure happiness. "You really care about her, don't you?" Ioana asked.

"I think she's magnificent," he said. "Every day she does some new thing I find entirely remarkable. And how are you doing?"

"Fine," Ioana said. She stared into Vampire Umpire's eyes and touched her lips with her fingers. "I'm going to be one of the ball girls on centre court in the New York tournament."

"That's really good," he said. "I'm doing a few night games on the second tier courts, but I'm told I'll be doing both the semi finals in the evening. And how are things with Jebediah?" He was standing with his arms crossed, and Ioana stood the same.

"It is not so good," she said. "I think the story of us must be ending soon."

"It is a trouble," he said. "But love is the finest thing in life, and I think when you find real, true love, it endures. So if it doesn't work out with him, it just means you're going to find someone perfect for you."

Ioana placed her hand around his lower back and planted a long kiss on his lips. He staggered and pushed her away. "You have a boyfriend," he said.

"I'm sorry," she said, and turned and left the stage area. He could feel the garlic scent clinging to his skin and he felt weak. He surreptitiously grabbed some melting ice surround a bucket that contained a medley of seafood and tried to wash his face. Then he walked over to Taylor, who was now alone.

♦

Molly and Taylor had talked for a while, though Molly was still star-struck enough that Taylor had done most of the conversational heavy-lifting. "So how did you meet Vampire Umpire?"

Molly told the story and after answering it, she found herself able to talk more easily. They spoke about what Taylor's music meant to Molly, and that was private to her and not for repeating. Taylor noticed Molly kept looking over at Vampire Umpire. "He's a good guy, isn't he?"

"He's okay," Molly said.

"He's the best," Taylor said. "It would be quite something to be loved by him, I think."

"Oh, it's not like that," Molly said.

"Are you sure? It's one of those things, isn't it? Sometimes we don't know how we feel until we've had one of those sleepless nights, spent pointlessly wondering how they think about us, or how they interpreted all the stupid things we said because we were too scared to say what we really wanted to."

As they watched, Ioana kissed Vampire Umpire. "I gotta go pee," Molly said.

"Of course," said Taylor. She watched as Vampire Umpire's silhouette made its way across the room to her. He moved like a falling rainstorm, she thought. Such grace, but such terrible restrained power.

◆

In the bathroom, Molly sat in the stall, thinking. She didn't know why she was feeling as she did. Probably some of the shrimp she had eaten were bad, she decided, but there seemed more to it than that. In any case, she didn't want to waste any time when she could be around Taylor Swift, so she composed herself and left the bathroom.

Outside, the cheers of the crowd still roared: few had gone home, with most hoping for the chance to see their idol leave the venue. The PA system was unleashing a playlist of Taylor Swift's favourite songs, mainly indie records by artists like The National, Sleater Kinney and Joanna Newsom. She could hear the excellent songs swell in volume as she walked along the dark corridor back to the room where the party was being held. And she failed to hear the person step up behind her and stab her in the side.

◆

Taylor and Vampire Umpire were chatting when he scented with his vampire sense of smell Molly's blood in the air. "Go to your dressing room, now," he told Taylor and instantly used all his speed to get to his friend. Blood was oozing slowly out onto the ground and she wasn't moving. He checked her pulse.

It was steady, and the wound was not in a bad location. He tore his exquisitely tailored white shirt and used it as a bandage to stop the bleeding, then with his hypnotic powers of influence induced a woman in the party room to call an ambulance. He sat with Molly until they arrived. They took control of her care then.

"Are you family?" the paramedics asked him.

"No," he said, as he intended to be at the hospital long before the ambulance arrived to prepare the staff, and so had no desire to ride in it.

Once they left, he went to Taylor's dressing room to tell her what had happened and why he had to leave. But when he arrived, though the guard at the door said only Taylor had entered and no-one had left, the room was totally empty. Only the scent of flowers, coming from no source he could see, hung in the air.

Chapter Nineteen

When Molly woke, Vampire Umpire was sitting by the bed in a large wingback chair. The window was behind the chair, and he hunched within it for shade from the light surrounding them.

"You should have left me before dawn," she said.

"I was staying here until you woke, no matter what." He sniffed. "And now I'm trapped, anyway. Did you see who did it?"

"No," she said. "They attacked me from behind, like an American college freshman trying to get a date."

'That's pretty bleak."

"But also a striking social commentary, right?"

"Oh yeah, I'm proud of you. It has highlighted a feminist issue affecting college campuses everywhere but in a darkly humorous way that will make the message even more effective."

"Thank you," Molly said and smiled. She stretched in the bed and winced as the action of her muscles stressed the edges of her injury.

"It's an odd wound," Vampire Umpire said. "Not the kind of knife normally found used in crimes in New York. Quite a narrow blade, with only a mild point and just one cutting edge, like an old tanto or an athame."

Tyrone Ennis bustled into the room, with Jean and Ham Remington following close after. "My god, are you okay?" he asked.

"I mean I wouldn't mind some kind of pudding," Molly said. "But that's the main pain I'm feeling right now: the agony of hunger."

"You're my hero," Vampire Umpire said. "You're probably the bravest person in this hospital."

"Well what about Jean, wandering around everywhere with that haircut?" Molly asked.

Jean's hair was now cut short and ragged and spackled with coppery highlights.

"Aww, Molly, she probably got it torn out fighting a supernatural monster," Vampire Umpire said. "Judging by her hair, I'd say it was an aswang: its talons would have torn her hair when it tried to steal her face, and its acrid spit would have streaked it."

"Actually it was Fitzpatrick's on 39ᵗʰ Street," Ham said, helpfully. "The world's only combination Irish bar and hair salon."

"Thanks a lot, Ham," Jean said angrily. "How would you feel if I told them all about your new pedicure. BECAUSE I JUST DID. He has gloss lacquer on his toenails," she finished.

"Please, please," Tyrone Ennis said. "We have drifted off topic considerably. Ms. Durand, I will withdraw you from the New York tennis competition this week, with no fault so you won't lose your appearance fee."

"Wait, wait," Molly said. "Why am I withdrawn?"

"Well, your injury? Your doctor told me you are to use no more than forty percent of your capabilities for the next two weeks."

"Maybe you are the one who should be seeing a doctor… of the brain," Molly said. "Because you're saying crazy things right now."

"You got stabbed," Tyrone Ennis said. "If the knife had gone even a few centimetres deeper, you might have died. I can't in good conscience let you play."

"Jeez," Molly said, indignant. "I lived in Scotland for years: I'm not going to take time off just because of a stab wound."

"Plus even at forty percent, she'll still definitely win anyway," Vampire Umpire added. He was still hunched over in the chair, but now he steepled his fingers and looked at Molly with a smile.

"Thanks, Vampire Slump-ire," Molly said. "I wanted to say that but I like to seem like I'm modest and humble some times. Speaking of which, where is Taylor Swift?"

"Later," Vampire Umpire said.

"So you will play?" Tyrone Ennis asked.

"When is my first match?"

"Tomorrow," he said. "At noon."

"Cool," said Molly. "So after I win my match I can have a Five Guys for lunch. I always get one of every milkshake," she confided to the room.

"An athlete always needs a big meal after a competition," Tyrone Ennis said.

"What are you talking about? That's my regular order."

"Yeah, I'm sure it won't be the first time you've had five guys all up in your mouth," Jean said, clearly still aggrieved about the haircut incident.

"Yeah right, Jean," Molly said. "From what Ham told me you've swallowed more guys than the whale in Pinocchio."

Jean turned on Ham with a look of fury and Tyrone Ennis rapidly interposed himself between the siblings, displaying quite some courage considering the murderous intent she displayed. "Now, now, enough," he said. "You're meant to be protecting my tennis players, not hurting each other."

"Sorry Mr. Ennis," they both said, Ham in particular hanging his head like meat being cured.

"And I'm not too happy with your performance," he continued. "Ms. Durand and Vampire Umpire have had several attempts on their lives and you still haven't found the vampire attacking the tour. But we shall discuss this outside, as we are disturbing Ms. Durand. Vampire Umpire, would you like a lift to the stadium of tennis? I believe you are umpiring in a couple of hours."

"I'll make my own way," Vampire Umpire said. "I want to spend a little more time with Molly first." Once he heard, with his vampire senses, Tyrone Ennis and the Remington siblings entering the elevator at the other end of the ward, he picked up his phone. "This'll just take a moment," he told Molly. "Hi, Blake Sennett? I'm Vampire Umpire, the human umpire at your tennis match this afternoon?"

"Hi Vampire Umpire," Blake said. "Everything okay for the match?"

"It sure is," he said. "It is a lovely clear day with the sun blazing down hot on the court. By the way, parenthetically and apropos of nothing, I just read an article in, ummm, Popular Culture magazine that said you were currently attractive to members of whichever sex it is to which you are attracted, but that if you became more tanned that attraction would diminish considerably."

"I see," said Blake. "I think I am becoming sick and will need to play later in the day once the sun goes down."

"That is fair. Good day to you Blake Sennett. It was nice talking to you."

"I also enjoyed your conversation. Goodbye and I will see you later."

Vampire Umpire called the other player. "Hello Quincy Hanley," he said. "I just wanted to see if you were ready for the tennis match this afternoon."

"I am ready," Quincy Hanley said. "I'm going to take the other guy to scHool."

"That is good, assuming you mean that as trash talk and not an earnest desire to reenrol the other player in some kind of educational institution."

"I most certainly mean the former," Hanley said.

"Then I shall see you this afternoon. Although I just met a witch who told me that the goddess Diana would favour you in the encounter if you played it under her silvery light."

"You did?" Hanley asked, clearly curious. "I mean, I don't believe in superstition. But," he fake coughed twice. "I feel like I'm sick and won't be fully healed and able to play until later tonight."

"That is understandable and just. I will call and say both players need to change the time of the match, so you won't have to forfeit. A pleasant afternoon to you and thanks for taking time to answer my call."

"Conversation with you is a pleasure I would never deny myself," Hanley said. "Good day and I will speak to you soon again I hope." Again, they both hanged up their respective phones, as hanging up each other's would have suggested a proximity that obviated the need for telephonic communication.

"You play humanity like Prince played literally every musical instrument ever created," Molly said. "Virtuousically and well."

"I suppose I was a little manipulative," Vampire Umpire said. "But really I am protecting them from dehydration, competing in heat like this."

"So what happened to Taylor Swift?" Molly asked. "Is she okay?"

"She has gone missing," Vampire Umpire said. "And tonight at midnight may be our last chance to get her back."

"What?" Molly asked, her voice breaking with the weight of concern. "Where is she?"

"I will tell you tonight," Vampire Umpire said. "If I am wrong, I will look really stupid and I don't want that to happen."

"I mean, I'm obviously hugely curious," Molly said. "But I also respect you and your desire to keep your dignity."

♦

That evening, after his match, Vampire Umpire and Molly walked the streets of New York to a gutter bar where he hoped to find the information he would need. In an ill-lit backroom he handed a nameless man in a flat cap and a ratty jacket stained in beer and whiskey shades a smallish wad of folded notes. "I'm looking for a fairy ring," he told the man.

"Awww, jeez, dude, that ain't cool," the snitch said. "It's the twenty first century. You can't use language like that anymore. However, you paid me so I guess I can recommend to you this place I know called Circle Jerks. It is a nightly gathering of amorous but slightly rude gay men. They'll handle whatever business you bring them."

Once Vampire Umpire explained that he wanted exactly what he had said, and that any latent homophobia had been inherent to his listener and not his speech, the snitch hesitantly offered them a different piece of advice. "It's not really my area. There's an old monument in central park, I guess? In the woods past the zoo." He entered the GPS coordinates into Vampire Umpire's phone.

As they walked to the location, Molly said, "Okay, you need to tell me what's going on now."

"All the problems Taylor had been having," Vampire Umpire said, "sounded like someone being cursed by faeries. And when I went into her room, the scent left behind was the rich stench of the jungle of the Seelie Court."

"But there's no such thing as fairies," Molly said.

"Spoken like a true republican," Vampire Umpire said. "But isn't there also no such thing as vampires?"

"Doesn't one die every time you say that?"

"We're all already dead, remember?"

"So what's the plan?"

"Well we're going to try to cross over into the faerie realm tonight at midnight, when the walls between worlds are thinnest. Then we'll just see what happens."

"Good plan."

◆

As the clocks approached midnight, Molly and Vampire Umpire stood outside a circle of standing stones about two metres across. Each stone was carved crudely into a rough cuboid and inlaid with tangled Celtic knots. Other than the moon, no light illuminated the scene. "What now?" Molly asked.

"We have to make an offering," Vampire Umpire said, and he walked around the stones, leaving atop each a fun-size American-style Milky Way.

"Sweets?" Molly asked.

"Well, different worlds value different things. Over there you'll find more diamonds than a Scotchman has crabs, but candy is rarer than gold."

"I'm more concerned that there aren't going to be any left for me."

"Well, I did buy two bags. And also, I kind of feel like if you have to make a choice between maybe saving your hero's life and having a snack that should not be too big a struggle."

"You're right, gimme the milky ways." She lunged at him fast.

Molly grabbed for the bag of sweets and Vampire Umpire tried to wrestle them away from her without re-opening her cut. "No, give them back," he was shouting at the exact moment midnight struck and suddenly the circle of stones simply was no longer present. Instead two worlds seemed to waver in place, rippling from one to the other. One moment the skyline of New York – countless glimmering diamonds of light outdoing the black night sky; and the next a world of tangled vines and murk-filled pools, with trees rearing high into a deep purple vault of heaven studded with several moons.

Vampire Umpire held Molly's hand and strode boldly into the new world. Instantly she found herself tugged down hard to the ground, and she looked to her right, where Vampire Umpire was sinking fast into a glutinous, crimson mud. "Did you just fall into that?"

"I didn't see it when we walked through," he said.

"Poor ol' Swampire Umpire," Molly said. "So clumsy."

"Would you mind helping me out? Both literally and figuratively?"

"In a minute or two," Molly said. "I want to take a few photos and demean you some more first."

Eventually she did extract him from the pool, once she had consumed more than a few of the lagniappe milky ways, and they looked around. The trees dwarfed any on earth. Their diameter was easily three of Molly's paces, and they grew so tall the tops were lost to the night. They were spattered with thick golden leaves lined with silver veins, and the water held in a few of these was a sweet nectar that smelled faintly of wine.

"I know a few alcoholics who would *love* this," she said, after touching a drop to her tongue.

"Do you mean you?"

"Hey, I only drink so I can tolerate your company," she said, winking at him.

"Don't consume anything else here," he said. "They can be weird about stuff like that."

"So it's like going for tea at an elderly aunt's house? They might be generous but there's a faint suspicion that everything might also be soaked in urine?"

"That's right: just politely refuse anything they offer and hold your nose as much as you can without seeming impolite."

Now he mentioned it, the smell of the world was overwhelming. It was floral in the same way as a cheap perfume: so overpowering it seemed almost artificial. Large flowers in a strange mix of colours dotted the landscape, Molly saw. But they seemed more to merge with the ground than grow from it: where one form encountered another it seemed to blend into it, like paint smeared while it was drying on a painting. The whole world, she realised, had this strange effect. Overhead the largest moon, which was striated in green and yellow, trailed slowly through the sky leaving a pale wash of those colours behind it, like a watercolour.

"This way," Vampire Umpire said, sniffing the air, and he lead them along through the forest.

"How do you know?" she asked.

"I can smell her," he said.

◆

In time they arrived at a clearing within which stood a gargantuan structure made of several of the colossal trees warped around each other. The gnarled branches and roots of the trees were wound together in some impossible way such that room-sized spaces formed all around the central stalk and hung from it like acorns from an oak. Fronds of vinous material delineated roofs and the golden leaves marked windows, Molly realised, as she could see several twitched back and forth as they approached.

All around them, the world's inhabitants flitted with an absolute indifference to their presence. In low light, many would have passed for human – they had the correct number of limbs and an approximation of the usual facial features – but they were far slighter and more etiolated, and their skin was shaded in every hue of the spectrum. Others had more arms, or features that merged human and animal in ways that were often savage or unsettling but always beautiful. Many, circling high above, had wings like birds or bees in style if not in scale.

Vampire Umpire stopped one of the faeries. It was vermillion-skinned, with four arms, each ending in a hand adorned with only a thumb and two fingers. "I am looking for a human brought here recently," he said. "Her name is Taylor Swift."

"And if you can outwit me," the creature said, "then your reward is within my gift." Its voice was low and musical, like a lyre softly strummed.

"How do we outwit you?" Molly asked. "Can I just use my fists?"

"Victory lies in the brain pan," the faerie said, "and not at the end of your wrists."

"So do you want to have some kind of smartness competition?" she asked. "What would be the rules?"

"If I fed on thoughts you'd leave me with inanition, for the two of you are fools."

"Why you rude little ass," she said.

"My test you will not pass," it told her.

"Hold on," Vampire Umpire said, placing a hand on Molly's arm. "It's a rhyme game. We need to find a phrase it can't rhyme, I think."

The faerie smiled and said, "I can't answer if you're right or wrong for I am far from tame, but if you watch my face you'll see at your recent notion I wink."

"Ohhhh," said Molly. "Then no worries Vampire Umpire. I got this." She stepped square to the faerie and said, "Hey faerie, would you mind getting me an orange?"

The faerie's brow furrowed in thought and it began to waver. Molly nodded confidently at Vampire Umpire, who immediately said, "Did you know that a spore case is known as a sporange?" Their foe immediately settled.

"Whaa? Why would you do that?" Molly asked Vampire Umpire, aghast.

"I mean, I know that fact and I never get the chance to use it," he said. "Sorry, but I can't regret my decision."

"Unbelievable. Okay, let me try this instead." Once again she tested her foe, this time with "I would say the sky is purple."

For long moments the faerie thought, and finally it spoke. "At night when I get lonely I like to stroke my nurples."

"Nurples?" Molly asked.

"Yeah, nurples doesn't count," Vampire Umpire said.

"God, I know," the faerie said. "I just got stuck and I figured if I said it confidently I'd get away with it."

"Well you didn't buddy," Molly said. "Lead on."

"For the record," Vampire Umpire said, "Hirple, meaning to walk with a limping motion, rhymes with purple." He looked at Molly shyly, seeking approval. "I didn't say that until after you won, even though I wanted to."

"You are such a nerd," she said.

◆

Their companion led them before the Faerie Queen. Her skin was green and cracked all over like bark. Her eyes were pure mercury and seemed to flow about her face at her merest whim. Her hair was a wispy contour of grey cloud. When she spoke, her slow, deep voice seemed to come less from her body and more from the slow creaking of the branches that made up her throne room. "What do you wish here?" she said.

"We have come for our friend," Vampire Umpire said. "And we will not leave her here with you."

"Your friend belongs to me," the Queen intoned sternly. "And for all time she will dwell by my side."

"Why does she belong to you?" Molly said. "Everyone should be free." She turned that to Vampire Umpire and added, "I learned that from a movie I saw once called Django Unchained. I think it was about the high price of slaves and how they were pricing themselves out of the market, the way maybe Apple are with their laptops."

"I think you have misunderstood that movie but made some salient points about Apple's increasingly untenable business model," Vampire Umpire replied, softly.

The queen interrupted their colloquy. "She made a deal, ten of your years ago. For a decade her songs would enrapture the world because imbued with my faerie music, and then she would be mine for ever."

"That doesn't sound right," Molly said. "First of all her music has a pretty earthly quality. It's less about being mystically beautiful than about conveying honest feelings with clever lyrics and catchy melodies. And secondly I don't think she'd do that. It doesn't seem like her."

"Yeah," said Vampire Umpire. "I dated her for a while and she certainly never mentioned a faerie deal to me. And nor did I detect the taint of your people on her skin, as all the mortals with which you make deals are marked."

Molly frowned. "Just had to remind me you dated her, huh?"

"Dated her *thoroughly*," Vampire Umpire said, and winked. "Like dated her all the way. Every way."

The queen paused. Her mercury eyes flowed from her face and out in a thin strand that sped out of the room. For a moment they stood watching and then with a flash the twin silver pools formed again on her face. "This is super awkward," the queen said. "It turns out I had intended to make the offer but never did. So this has been just a really big administrative error."

"Oh, right," said Molly. "So we're good?"

"Yeah, sorry," the queen said. "I will release her and you back into your world. Sorry for the hassle guys."

"No biggie," said Vampire Umpire. "It happens."

♦

They deposited Taylor Swift at her Manhattan home later that night. "If there is anything I can do for you, I will," she said. "I owe you two my life."

"You know I don't need anything," Vampire Umpire said, and they hugged.

"And do you want anything?" Taylor asked Molly. "You can have anything you like."

Molly knew there was only one thing she wanted. She wanted Taylor to write a song about her. But her throat was dry and she wanted to make her request clearly, so she said, "Could I have a glass of water please?"

"Sure," said Taylor. "I'll have my housekeeper bring you one. I'm exhausted and going to bed now, so let yourself out once you've drunk it. FAVOUR RETURNED," she shouted and high fived Molly, legally sealing the deal.

◆

"Was the water good at least?" Vampire Umpire asked as they walked to their hotel at four am along the cold New York streets.

"It was both cold and refreshing," Molly said. "But that doesn't really diminish the frustration inherent to that moment."

"You'll get over it in time."

"Do you think?"

"Yeah. A few years from now that memory will fade from your mind, leaving only a blank space."

Given the day she'd had, out of kindness Vampire Umpire decided not to avoid the punch Molly threw at his face.

Chapter Twenty

Molly spat the big bite of her burrito back into the brown paper bag, then tossed the bag into the back of the car, where it clattered hard into the bowl of the New York tennis tournament trophy. The trophy was made of gold and chimed like a bell when it was struck. The bag burst open and the burrito flew apart, filling the bowl with shredded lettuce, over-cooked meat and lumps of vaguely tomato-ish sauce. "That was disgusting," she said. "Drive back so I can complain."

"I can't just 'drive back'," Vampire Umpire complained. "We're on a motorway."

Molly looked behind them. "It's fine, there's nothing coming. Pull a U-ey."

"I'm really not meant to, I think."

"Okay, so just get into the slip road and we'll reverse back."

"For like four miles?" Vampire Umpire gripped the wheel firmly and looked over. "You want me to reverse along the slip road for four miles? Actually," he said, looking at the odometer, "five now."

"So if we've learned anything, it's that the sooner you do it, the less reversing you're going to have to do."

"But what do you think will happen?"

"Well they'll hopefully give me another burrito," Molly said.

"Another bad burrito. Which…?"

Molly thought for a moment and then her face went semen-pale with horror. "Which I would then have to eat." She clenched her fingers around Vampire Umpire's forearm. "Please don't take us back there," she begged. "I don't want to have to eat more bad burrito."

"Okay, fine," he said. "I have given up on the idea entirely."

They were driving from Los Angeles down interstate ten to the next tennis engagement, at Indian Wells. After New York, they'd flown out to LA and rented a car. The intention had been to get a hotel there for a couple of nights, but when Molly saw the prices she had insisted they leave at once, reasoning that the tennis centre would be cheaper and maybe even let her stay for free.

It was only a bit over one hundred miles and Vampire Umpire had, despite never legally obtaining a license, a desire to drive, so she had let him. They were in the desert now, and in the night it was cold and empty as a bad dog's heart. Molly queued up some driving music on her iPod and they drove on under more stars than either had ever seen.

"How come the light of the sun would kill you," Molly said, "but the light from billions of stars, all of them suns, does nothing?"

"It's only specific wavelengths of light that injure vampires," Vampire Umpire said. "And actually all of the stars are either red or blue shifted as they travel towards or away from us, so those wavelengths are no longer present in their spectra."

"Is that true?" Molly asked.

"Probably. I mean, could you tell me how every detail of your body works?"

"Well most of it. Except when I am doing my toilet business. I want nothing to do with that."

"So there you go."

◆

It was past three in the morning when they arrived in Indian Wells. The town was entirely asleep: no cars nor lights disturbed the night, and no-one walked the streets. The tennis centre was completely blacked out, so Vampire Umpire was eventually able to convince Molly to let him take her to a hotel.

They pulled into the parking lot and walked up to the glass door. Reception was deserted, but the door opened when they pushed. They stood at the desk for a moment before Molly said, "That's long enough," and jammed her finger on the call button.

"I appreciate you waiting those nearly three seconds," Vampire Umpire said.

"Your patience is rubbing off on me like an insomniac boyfriend in the night," she said.

Her finger still pressed the buzzer, but no-one was appearing.

"This place seems deserted," Vampire Umpire said.

"Yeah, it's like one of your birthday parties," she said.

"Oh yeah, well where's the cake then?" Vampire Umpire asked.

"Damn it," Molly said. "Now I really really want cake."

"You don't want to mess with me," he said. "It's a lesson."

"You're right," she replied. "I've only made myself sad."

They wandered about the lobby, checking the hotel bar where they found only bad lighting, no staff and a bottle of rum, which Molly deftly pinched. Still no-one showed up. "I guess we try somewhere else?" she said.

But the next hotel proved exactly the same, and the one after that was locked shut and no matter how hard Molly leaned on the bell no response was to be found. By this time, the sun was beginning to threaten the horizon, and Molly was beginning to worry about Vampire Umpire, as the only people who responded worse to sunlight than him were gingers.

"Let's just go to the tennis centre," she said. "I'll wait until they open and you can sleep in the boot."

"I mean, usually my plan would be to break in somewhere, but I guess sleeping in the boot on top of the spare tyre is just as good."

"Hey, I dated a fat guy once and let me tell you," Molly said, "a spare tire can be *comfortable*."

"Then how come you aren't together anymore."

"I like to be able to out-eat anyone I date," she said. "It's like a dominance thing."

◆

When she woke, the dashboard clock claimed it was just past two in the afternoon. Her mouth was sticky from stewing too long in the sun, and her head hurt. She fished around in the debris under her seat until she found her bottle of water, which she chugged. Still thirsty, she decided it was time to go in to the centre to see if they had free water for tennis champions. Otherwise she could just go to the bathroom and steal some water from the taps.

She felt groggy, and the quiddity of the world only barely impinged her awareness. It was odd that no-one had disturbed her while she slept in their car, she thought, and somewhere she realised that for a tennis centre about to host an international tournament there was very little activity. She walked through the abandoned cars in the parking lot, squinting against the sun and idly tapping her bottle lightly against the side of her leg.

Once more, the front desk was abandoned, and she began to feel almost like she was in a dream. There was a drinking fountain though, and she placed her emptied bottle against the nozzle and refilled it. She bent over to drink directly from it, and she noticed a thick smear of dried red fluid on the edge of silver top. It looked like a trailed hand print. She bent down so her head was level with the waist-high fountain, and she could she the trail continued down off the silver onto the black plastic of the pedestal.

She felt a momentary prickle of fear caress the base of her spine, and she spun quickly, expecting to see someone behind her. But she was still entirely alone. She settled herself; probably someone had cut themselves on the metal of the fountain, or something similar. But still, she walked into the pro shop and grabbed one of the heavier racquets off the shelf. It was the original Wilson Pro Staff RF97, and she trailed her finger idly over the criss-cross red and black pattern as she moved deeper into the centre.

In the male locker room she heard a running faucet, but when she called out and stepped into the shower, hoping at best to see some hot dude's dong and at worst to see at least a person, she found only steam so thick she could almost chew it and a heat more oppressive than the desert. The female locker room was abandoned entirely and deathly silent as the audience after Ed Sheeran has perpetrated one of his sonic atrocities.

In the office suites, the only thing preventing the area from seeming like a posed photograph for a supply company were the piles of paper abandoned on the floor and trodden over by massed feet. She waggled the mouse at one of the computers and she saw someone had been working on designing some graphic for the tournament, with a picture of Molly's face and a list of her wins this season, but simply abandoned it.

She walked through the upper levels towards the doors into the stadium. She was just pushing them open when someone grabbed her shoulder. "Don't!" a voice hissed in her ear. "They'll hear you."

"Oh, are they playing already?" Molly asked. It didn't make sense to her, but tennis players hated any interruption or noise during their games. She sometimes sang sweet but deranged songs of her own creation to herself as she played, to avoid boredom. She saw that the person who had stopped her was a man. He was dressed in badly torn black Levi jeans and a t-shirt that had read 'Welcome to Indian Wells' but now had been daubed crudely with red to instead display "Hellcomes to Indian Wells.'

"Playing? Are you insane? They're all down there."

"All the other tennis players? Did I sleep through the opening ceremony again?" Molly thought about consoling the man with the classic old pat on his shoulder but, given the dishevelment of his garb and the stench of BO that clung about him like sycophants around a celebrity, decided against it. "Don't worry, I'll just make a quiet entrance. Realll easy like." She pushed towards the door and he grabbed her again.

"Jeez, let go Grabby Abby," she told him.

"You don't understand. You can't reason with them; they won't listen to you. All they want is destruction. They're sick, mindless monsters with neither soul nor conscience."

"Oh my god," said Molly. "You mean…?"

"Yes," the man said, nodding and looking relieved.

"So the whole stadium is filled with Trump voters?" Molly scowled. "Good, I've been wanting to give those morons a piece of my mind for a few seconds now." Before the man could stop her she stepped out into the light.

The first clue that they weren't Trump voters was that many of the… people in the stadium were thin and well-dressed, and many were even not white. The stench of rotting meat could go either way, after all. There were a handful of common features to all of them: their eyes were entirely white, with no iris or pupil. Their fingers were grimy with dried gore, many now just bone shards jutting from their palms, some with long and torn nails barely clinging to their flesh. The skin of many in the crowd was beginning to peel, and hung off in long ragged strips.

"Not Trump voters," the man whispered to her from the shadows of the door behind which he cowered. "Zombies."

"Please," said Molly. "Like there's a difference." Unfortunately, she spoke at normal volume and as one all the heads in the stadium turned to face her. She paused. One of the zombies nearest her, she noticed, was missing his lower jaw, and his tongue hung down into empty space like a thick, hideous neck tie, the kind you might buy from Primark. "How y'all doing?" she said, and waved.

The horde began to move towards her. "Follow me," the man said, and grabbed her arm. He pulled her along with him down the corridor. The zombies followed, slow but inexorable as a tide undercutting a cliff. He ducked through a side door and slammed it behind them, then began pushing a large filing cabinet against the door. Molly helped and moments before they were done, the door began to reverberate with the clamour of the zombies' fists.

Looking around, Molly realised they were in a security room. A long bank of monitors lined one wall, and on another were a series of uniforms. "Any weapons?" she asked the man.

"None. We don't even have tasers."

"Man," said Molly. "Who'd have thought a *lack* of guns would be a problem in America?"

The filing cabinet rocked but settled back, and Molly and the man added a second one to brace it. "They're going to get in," the man said, and she could hysteria rising in his voice like a well-yeasted dough. Molly hefted the racquet she was still holding. It was better than nothing she guessed.

"I'm Molly," she said. "Who are you?"

She was vaguely irritated that he had no clue who she was, but it turned out the man's name was Logan Bechdel and he had been hired as a guide for the tournament and had no interest in tennis, which she guessed gave them a commonality that might perhaps provide a basis for friendship. He explained that three days before, staff had suddenly started attacking each other randomly, and that everyone bitten or scratched or who in some way shared fluids with one of the zombies became one of them.

"Shared fluids?" Molly asked.

"Well some people are really lonely."

"I guess that's a truly paranormal romance," Molly said. "So you've been hiding out since then? Why not try to get away?"

Bechdel explained that the zombies had spread all across town, though the bulk had clustered at the tennis centre, possibly because their love for tennis survived even death. As he spoke, a crack began to appear in the wood of the door. The man began to shake and clutched his fingers over his mouth, from which moans came like Kim Kardashian when they don't shut down a store in which she is shopping, or Kim Kardashian when Kanye's doing it real nice, if he ever even does. He's been bitten too, Molly thought, and was about to destroy the man's brain more thoroughly than a video game when she heard his tears splash on the floor and realised he was just crying.

"These monitors," Molly said. "Can you show me the first attack?"

"Why?" he said.

Mainly, she wanted to give him something to do to distract him from the situation, but she felt telling him that might kind of spoil the placebo effect for which she was aiming. "I really love gore," she said. "But I also hate spoilers. So we'll see the first one then go from there."

While he searched through the archive, Molly piled up as much furniture as she could around the increasingly only hypothetical door. First it was just the low moaning choir of the zombies that came through and then she found herself having to avoid swipes from their claws if she got too near. Finally, one of them managed to get his head through the door, which didn't work so well after she ploughed her racquet through it. Most of the zombie's blood had coagulated and was black as the new moon, so she didn't mess up her racquet. She paused to congratulate herself on her choice. It was an amazing racquet, and if Wilson wanted to maybe sponsor her, or anyone else, they'd be more than welcome.

"I've got it," Bechdel said, right as the door collapsed completely. The zombies began to seep into the room. Bechdel cowered on the floor well behind Molly, who slammed her racquet down on skull after skull. The zombies were slow, and she fought long, but their numbers seemed infinite and her arms grew heavier and heavier until she felt no more could she lift them.

She and Bechdel backed into the far corner of the room. With all her will applied she could still lift the racquet, but when she swung it now it didn't cleave the enemy as it once had, and the horde was only swayed back for brief and ever decreasing moments. They surrounded her completely now, and they were too many for there to be any hope of escape. She could feel the breath of the nearest zombie cold and rancid against her cheek, like a gust of decayed meat that someone keeps storing in a fridge out of confusion.

Chapter Twenty-One

Molly saw the zombie's teeth closing in on her eye and she slammed her fist hard into its torso. It fell back, but the weight of dead flesh pushing behind it soon forced it in contact again. She punched her fists against it, over and over, as fast as she could, but her strength was spent and it was like a butterfly's wings flapping against the skin of an angry tyrannosaurus. It went for her throat this time.

Suddenly the zombie's head was yanked back, and she saw it flying off to bounce against the distant wall. In her perception the next few moments saw the near literal liquidation of the entire horde by some kind of blur, which resolved itself into the shape of her Vampire Umpire.

The sun had set a few minutes before, and Vampire Umpire, cramped in the confines of the car trunk had eagerly opened it and stepped out to stretch in the night. After a moment, the strange charnel smell of the area had piqued his sensitive nostrils, and shortly after he began scent-trailing Molly to ensure she was okay. When his vampire senses detected the sound of the attacking zombies, he abandoned the cautionary semblance of normal speed and raced to the security room.

Even before he realised it, he was attacking them with a ferocity he had never before known. With all his strength, he swept them aside like bowling pins from a ball who believed the pins to be sleeping with his wife in some weird way, possibly by inserting the heads of the pins into her finger holes? I dunno, I haven't thought about it all that much. It's definitely not a fetish of mine. Still, he tried to hurt none of them terminally, until he saw one about to hurt Molly.

He grabbed the zombie by the head and yanked back, but his strength tore the skin apart like a desperately hungry man opening the over-complicated packaging of a Kinder Bueno. With the force of the blow, the zombie's greasy hair slipped through his fingers and clattered hard off the wall. It rebounded and bounced off the face of the other man in the room. He looked simultaneously terrified and offended.

Molly safe, Vampire Umpire drove the zombies out of the room and then grabbed the heavy filing cabinets, crushed them together and drove them hard into the vacated door frame. Finally, he stopped, and said, "Hey, you guys okay?"

"I mean," Molly said, "I'm a bit annoyed it took you so long to save our lives."

"That was inconsiderate of me, I'm sorry."

"Were you distracted by the Pac-Man machine in the lobby?"

"I thought you knew me, Molly. It is Ms. Pac-Man whose siren song I cannot resist."

"I actually think it is a Ms. Pac-Man machine," said Bechdel. "I remember because I accused the manager of being sexist. There should be equal opportunities for men as well as women."

"Yep, that is the exact point of equality," Vampire Umpire said. "Making sure that the centuries of oppression of men by the women that have constantly and overwhelmingly occupied every position of power gets rectified." The level of sarcasm in his voice was so deep only a vampire with millennia of practice solely in the art of the sarcastique could have hoped to equal it.

"Pac-Men have rights, too, Vampire Umpire," Molly said. Simultaneously, though, she swiped idly with her racquet at a mug on the security desk, which – perhaps accidentally, though it seems unlikely given her accomplishments as a tennis player

– smacked meatily into Bechdel's foot and shattered. "Ooops," she said, with a stunning lack of concern.

"Alright," Bechdel said, after a few moments of hopping had diminished the pain of his possibly splintered toes. "I've seen every zombie movie ever made."

"Nerd!" Molly interrupted.

"Oh for god's sake. Zombie movies are cool now," he said.

"I don't think so," said Vampire Umpire. "I think there was a brief resurgence after 28 Days Later and then the ensuing sub-mediocrity of all the films that followed meant it was only really conceptually cool."

"How do you mean, conceptually cool?" Molly asked.

"I think that online opinion creates a kind of hypothetical excitement for things that often isn't realised actually. Like a kind of cargo cult effect, except people seize on something as a cultural signifier, until the lack of actual quality examples of the thing means the opinion becomes unsustainable."

"Like how everyone thought Snakes on a Plane would be amazing and hilarious but actually it just sucked?" Molly said.

"Yeah, exactly like that."

"Snakes on a Plane was amazing!" Bechdel protested.

"You run a film blog, don't you?"

"So?" Bechdel said. Vampire Umpire had never killed anyone, but increasingly now he wondered if it would have been highly unethical just to not save this one guy.

"I guess we all are entitled to our opinions," Vampire Umpire said.

"I got this t-shirt," Bechdel said. "It says, 'Opinions are like assholes: we all have one and they all stink.'"

"Not mine," said Molly. "I keep my butt clean as a particularly clean whistle."

"And mine never gets used," said Vampire Umpire. "But to descend to your level, maybe opinions are like shit – some are more efficiently formed and better composed than others."

Bechdel thought for a moment but had no response to this. Instead, he began stripping off his clothes.

"Whoa, whoa," Molly said. "You may be a nerd, but even you can't have thought that was foreplay."

"I'm referring back to the zombie movie thing!" he said. "In every movie, after an attack, someone asks if anyone got bitten. And everyone always says no, but someone is lying and they turn into a zombie. So this is the surest way of knowing."

"Yeaaaahhhhh," said Molly. "No-one gets to see me naked unless they pay."

"Uhhh," said Vampire Umpire. "Wow."

"TO TAKE ME TO DINNER, I MEANT," Molly yelled, Harry Potter style: all caps.

Bechdel was now standing only in his boxers, which were stained at the front in a dark, yellowish colour that did not look to be part of the original design of the fabric. Molly ended up looking elsewhere somewhat desperately, and she saw the security footage still playing. "Hey, what's that?" she said.

"Oh, the first attack," Bechdel said. He was shivering slightly, and his hands were clasped in front of his body at penis level. "I was getting ready to show it to you."

On the screen one of the creatures was shambling towards the crowd of normal people, like a Mormon approaching their first victim of the day. "That's the original one," Bechdel said. "I've watched the tapes over and over. Had nothing else to do here."

"Too scared to masturbate?" Vampire Umpire asked.

"Ye... sorry, I didn't hear you," Bechdel said and blushed, over all of his body covered by neither his boxers nor his hands.

"But I meant this," Molly said. She pointed to the background of the image, where a van sat idling, its side door open.

"Run the tape back," Vampire Umpire said.

"It's really a file now," Molly said. "Video is now stored as digital files, without the clumsiness or friability of old magnetic tape."

"Thank you. I definitely didn't know that and was not just using a figure of speech for elegance of phrasing and convenience."

Bechdel sat down at the desk and Molly stood first close to his shoulder and then further back as his odour caught her nostrils. He scrolled the video back, and sure enough the zombie trailed its slow way backwards into the darkness of the side door, which closed behind it. He ran the video forward again and it emerged, with a little prompting from a foot.

"Run the tape back again," Molly said.

"It's really a file now," Vampire Umpire said.

"Hush," said Molly to him. "Do it, nerd," she said to Bechdel. Then she said, "Pause it." She pointed to the screen, where on the side door of the van were the words Casa de la Bruja and in smaller writing a website.

"I guess I can hack their website, then get their location from their IP address," Bechdel said.

"Hh," said Molly. "I'll tell you my IP address: any where there's a bathroom."

"Or we could just, y'know," Vampire Umpire said, "type the name into google maps and have it right here?" He placed his phone flat on the security table in front of them. "That's an LED backlit LCD capacitive touch screen, by the way, Molly: not a polaroid picture. In case you were wondering." Like fries from 5 Guys, Molly could tell Vampire Umpire was a bit salty.

◆

Molly and Vampire Umpire drove up the duckstone path to the house. The villa, a few miles outside Mexicali, reared up three stuccoed storeys in front of them, each window framed in dark mahogany and lit softly within by a lambent amber glow. Planter pots spilled over with a profusion of petals, and automatic lawn sprinklers deployed hosing down grass as green as a mint julep. Against the starry night sky palm trees dotted the grounds.

At the door, a butler led them to a terrace beside a swimming pool, where a man with jet black hair and a clearly all-over tan greeted them.

"Why did you do it?" Molly asked. "You killed all those people."

He smiled, beautifully. "And the plague of the dead will continue, all across the United States," he said. "Until the Mexican president will have to build a wall, to keep them out of here."

"So that's why you did it?" Molly asked. "You're part of that deranged scheme?"

"God no. I may, I accept, be mad. I do not think a sane man could survive what the North Americans did to me, nor would they take the revenge I have." He sipped the whiskey sitting by his hand. "But I had no choice."

"What did they do to you?" Vampire Umpire asked. "Who are you?"

"My name is Felix Navidad," said the man, who from now on I shall also refer to using some combination of Felix and/or Navidad. "And I was a great singer."

"I've never heard of you," said Molly. "And I've heard of every great singer: Taylor Swift, Harry Styles, and that's all of them."

"You would not have heard of me. I was popular here, in Mexico. And then… then I wrote a Christmas song. It was beloved here, fourteen million hits on YouTube. It went viral."

"Like that time I got thrush," Vampire Umpire said, and nodded. "It's rarely a good thing going viral."

"Indeed not, sir." He shivered. "I got invited on the big late night chat show in the United States, hosted by Damon Letterson, to perform my song at Christmas time. The crowd, they loved me before I sang a note, cheering my name and laughing with, I thought delight and pleasure untrammelled by the woes of the world."

"And then?" Molly asked.

"Then, well… My song was a Christmas song, called Handling Santa's Sack. Here in Mexico it is perfectly clear what I meant, but in America it had a horrible double meaning. Especially the line about squeezing his sack hard so he gives me my present faster."

"Eesh," said Molly. "That is unfortunate."

"Well, I speak your language with a degree of infelicity," Navidad protested. "It was only good that things rhymed. Though I will admit that I should have perhaps rephrased the bit about eagerly sucking on the candy cane when it popped out of his pouch."

"So they hated the song?"

"No, far worse," Felix Navidad protested. "They bought it in their millions, and they still play it every year on near every television show about Christmas."

"Then what's the problem?" Molly asked.

"They were appreciating it *ironically*," Felix Navidad said, and by the tears in his eyes, both Molly and Vampire Umpire could see his anguish was unfeigned. "All those billions in sales and royalties because they thought it was so bad it was good."

"So you're going to murder everyone in America with zombies because they made you a novelty pop star?" Molly asked. (Navidad corrected her with "North America," but she ignored his interjection.)

"I mean, a nation that votes in Donald Trump, are they not eagerly clamouring for death?" Vampire Umpire asked.

"It's a fair point," Molly said. "But not one to be making in front of the homicidal maniac with whom we are reasoning, I feel."

"It's true," said Vampire Umpire. "I guess sometimes my love for rhetoric gets in the way of our confrontations some times."

"Well don't feel bad – everyone has personality traits they need to work on," Felix Navidad said. "Like once I had a girlfriend tell me I was fat, so I used some of my wealth to get a personal trainer to tone my body, and a surgeon to give me a little liposuction, and a new girlfriend who might love me for who I am. The moment we stop growing is the moment we start to ossify as humans, and that is a form of death in life."

"That's all for you, Navidad!" Molly yelled, trying to get the atmosphere back on track. "We have come to stop you."

"You plan to arrest me?"

"We have told the police," said Vampire Umpire. "My phone transmitted your confession to them, as I suspected they would not believe Molly and I if we just turned up as strangers with an outlandish story." He turned his head and smiled, listening to the sounds on the cool night air – the birds settling and the animals lowing and the chirping of the crickets. "I can hear their sirens, coming from the city now."

"Fine," said Navidad. "We shall see how long I serve. But North America will still suffer. Unless…"

"Unless what?" Molly asked.

"The zombieism… It is a curse, and the curse I used, it can be lifted. The zombies cannot be saved, there is no cure for them. But I can bring about their end. They are lost, but the United States could be saved."

"Why would you tell us that?" Vampire Umpire asked.

"Because you have tried to stop me, and the only way to stop the zombies will probably kill you."

"He knows a great magician," Molly said. "I'm sure he could stop them." She paused. "But he's kind of an asshole, so maybe tell us how we could get you to do it first?"

"We'll decide after that," Vampire Umpire said.

"Follow me," Felix Navidad said.

♦

He led them into the house, inside which a wild bacchanal was convened. In every room people danced to disparate styles of music, and drank beverages of wild expense. Each room was themed differently, and some were filled with soft music and conversation, while others were all hard liquor and harder dancing and hardest of all was the boning going on. But in the basement, all the participants were masked, and the music was provided by a small orchestra at the far end of a deep pit.

"Ladies and gentleman of the masquerade," Navidad shouted. "I bring to you the latest challengers." The crowd turned to face Molly and Vampire Umpire, and Navidad took their hands and raised them high above their heads. For their ears only, he said, "If you survive, I swear I will break the curse."

A ladder was lowered into the pit, and Molly and then Vampire Umpire climbed down. The ladder was raised again, and they were so deep not even Vampire Umpire was sure he could leap out.

"There is a dance," Navidad intoned for the crowd's benefit, though they listened with the air of celebrants hearing a mantra, "so wild and passionate that they say Death himself fears to take the dancers." He clapped his hands, and the sides of the pit began to shiver: cunningly worked stone had concealed openings in seemingly solid walls.

From the apertures, animals began to pour. Poisonous snakes coiled out slow and mean, and scorpions lashed at the air with their tails. From opposite ends, panthers and lions roared low and prowled with aggressive ease towards them. Small guide lines in the floor of the pit directed the beasts' attentions towards the centre, where stood Molly and Vampire Umpire.

"We call this dance," said Felix Navidad, "The Tango de la Muerte." He raised his arms dramatically, and the orchestra began a wild, pulsing song.

"Take my hand," Vampire Umpire told Molly. "We can do this." Around them swarmed the venomous beasts. (This is an important distinction – animals that carry poison in fangs or stingers of some kind are venomous, ones poisonous to the touch are poisonous.)

He stood wide, and pulled her towards him. Her body crushed against his, and her knee curved graceful and natural into the space between his spread legs. Her right hand was clasped firmly in his soft right hand, and the pressure of his other arm around her waist felt like something she had always missed. She curled her arm around his back and felt the long smooth muscles under her fingertips.

With the lightest gesture of his hand, suddenly she was twirling around. She just let go, and her feet flowed beneath her as graceful as a river. She spun back and stopped and he swirled beautifully then grabbed her and they danced about the floor in wide sweeps.

He pulled her in again, and with both hands around her waist, she bent back. At the limits of her flexibility he lifted her, and she swung into the air, spinning head over heels only to be caught the instant before panic told her she would hit the ground, with him behind her now. Around them, the creatures and the audience both watched enraptured.

They were both panting when the dance finished, and she was intensely aware of his body cool and solid against hers. A light clean sweat sprung from her brow. She stared into his eyes and his pupils were huge and the irises had never seemed to sparkle so beautifully in the light before. She didn't know if she moved first, or him, but suddenly she was kissing him, and his lips felt right and true on hers.

Above, the audience burst into rapturous applause, even above which Navidad's words could be heard. "Beautiful," he shouted. "I will honour our deal."

But in truth, Molly sensed nothing other than the kiss.

Chapter Twenty-Two

Tyrone Ennis, great to whatever would be the correct degree grandson of Terrence Ennis (inventor of Tennis) and owner-operator of the International Tennis League, reached across the desk. He took Vampire Umpire's hand in both of his and shook it vigorously, the way a hungry dog shakes a rag it mistakenly believes contains food – at length and with an uncomfortable degree of wetness.

"Vampire Umpire, I want to congratulate you," he began, "on being by far the finest umpire on tour so far this year. You have made no incorrect calls, none of your decisions were overturned and overall you have the first perfect record of any umpire in league history." He released Vampire Umpire's hand and continued, "Other than a weird coincidence, where all your matches have taken place at night somehow, you have been beyond exemplary. In fact if you can continue this level of performance, you will be unquestionably the greatest umpire of all time." He stared deep into Vampire Umpire's eyes and said, "That's the kind of immortality that few will ever grasp, Vampire Umpire."

"Thank you, Mr. Ennis," Vampire Umpire said. "My method is simple: I just say whether the ball is in or not."

"If only every umpire had your eyes," Tyrone Ennis said. "If I had twenty of you keeping an eye on our balls we would all be an awful lot happier at the International Tennis League."

"I am just happy to be given the chance," Vampire Umpire said. "Being an umpire has been one of the cornerstone ambitions of my entire life, I believe."

"Well, that is what I wanted to talk to you about."

"Really? I find it hard to believe you are about to fire me."

"Gosh no," said Tyrone Ennis. "In fact quite the opposite. Tomorrow is the final of Wimbledon – the most prestigious match of the year. And I thought, 'who would be better to umpire it than my very best umpire?'"

"Tom Hanks maybe?" offered Vampire Umpire. "People love him, and he seems super nice."

"Actually yes, Tom Hanks would be good, but I don't know if he has your skill at calling tennis matches."

"We could test him?"

"I don't know if there is time before tomorrow, but I shall consider it for next year. But, for this year, would you consider doing it?"

"It would be culmination of all my… very long life's goals," Vampire Umpire said. "So yes, I would be delighted to do it."

"That's good, that's good," Tyrone Ennis said. He walked around his desk and sat down in the chair beside Vampire Umpire's. "There's just one thing," he said, and placed his hand lightly on Vampire Umpire's leg.

"Uhhh, I don't want to earn the job that way," Vampire Umpire said.

Tyrone Ennis blushed and lifted his hand quickly. "Oh no! I didn't mean it that way, I was just attempting consolation."

"You're sure? You're not just saying that because I rejected your advances?"

"God no. If I made advances you'd know," Tyrone Ennis said. "I have many incredible chat up lines, like the following." He cleared his throat and then said, "Excuse me are you a naturalist Pokémon game? Because I want a peek-at-you naked."

Vampire Umpire sat unmoved and then said, "And just to be clear, you're using that as an example of a chat up line you might use, not using it now to try to seduce me?"

"That is correct," Tyrone Ennis said.

"Okay then. So what is the problem?"

"Well Molly told me yesterday at lunch that the two of you had kissed. And obviously I can't let you umpire her match if there is going to be any conflict of interest."

"Oh, I can promise there won't be. I would only ever call the match fairly."

"Well but there would still be the *appearance* of impropriety," Tyrone Ennis said, with a note of wheedling entering his voice.

"So you're saying…"

"If you want to umpire the Wimbledon final, the greatest and most prestigious match any umpire can ever umpire, you will have to end any relationship you have with Molly."

"I see," Vampire Umpire said.

◆

Jean and Ham Remington had called a press conference that evening, and all International Tennis League employees had been requested to attend. Vampire Umpire had of course gone along out of politeness, and he had dragged Molly along with him, though she was somewhat reluctant.

"Seriously, dude," she said. "What are they going to announce? That Ham is a terrible kisser, or that Jean is going to fix her terrible haircut?"

"I doubt it will be either of those things," Vampire Umpire said. "Those both seem like really bad guesses, if you don't mind me saying."

"They were not sincere guesses! I was making deliberately bad examples for comic effect." She playfully punched him in the shoulder, and he let his body sway back a little, as if the force had actually moved him.

The room was full now, the press down the front and all their colleagues clustered around the room in dense knots determined by friendships and rivalries. "Listen, I have to tell you something," Vampire Umpire said, when Ham and Jean stepped onto the stage and Ham rapped his knuckles against the microphone.

"Is this on?" he screamed, inadvertently blowing out two of the speakers and setting a ringing in the ears of every person in the room. When the cacophony had settled, he said, "Jean and I have an announcement. Jean…" He gestured towards the microphone and Jean stepped forward.

"Thank you Ham. I am proud to say that our investigation has concluded and we can now announce the identity of the vampire that has been stalking and sometimes killing members of the tennis tour."

Ham now returned to the microphone. "The truth is," he said and then began coughing. He choked and Jean hammered on his back a few times. "Sorry," he eventually continued. "I have a really wet mouth, and sometimes I accidentally swallow my saliva down my lungs hole instead of my stomach hole. Does anyone remember what I was saying?"

"The vampire!" Vampire Umpire yelled out helpfully.

"Oh right," said Ham. "Thank you, Vampire Umpire. The identity of the vampire on the tour is… there is no such thing as vampires."

Without exception everyone in the room failed to react. Molly and Vampire Umpire for obvious reasons, everyone else because they had long assumed that there wasn't such a thing as vampires. Jean now took over again. "I'm going to give you a moment to accept that," she said, clearly following a pre-prepared script that had failed to anticipate the audience's total apathy. "This morning Ham and I broke into the murdered umpire's home, and we found checks paid to him… by Jebediah Moslius!"

Everyone in the room stared about, trying to find Moslius, but he wasn't in the room. "Investigating the match record, we believe they were payments made by Moslius for preferential calls during matches."

"Then what about the bite marks?" a reporter asked.

Ham held up a photo of Moslius' hand bling. He had circled the two diamonds in the gold. "We believe they are actually puncture wounds from being punched by this. The spacing seems to match."

Jean said, "Once Moslius is arrested the police can check for residual blood and do all the necessary tests."

"Uhhh," said Molly. "You mean you didn't already have him arrested."

"No," said Jean, flushing slightly. "We felt it was more important to expose him quickly, before the police got involved."

"Because the police don't have your skill at arresting criminals?" said Molly.

"For shame," said Vampire Umpire. "I never thought you would be so into self-promotion Ham."

"I'm sorry, Vampire Umpire," Ham said. "It was mainly Jean's idea."

"We have to live according to our best impulses," said Vampire Umpire. "We should rise to the best in ourselves, and not buckle to the baser impulses of others."

Ham asked one of the journalists for a pad of paper and noted this down, and all involved felt it best to bring the press conference to an end.

◆

Molly and Vampire Umpire ran into Ioana outside the conference chamber. She was leaning against the wall and breathing hard. "Hard news to here, Ioana?" Vampire Umpire asked. She looked at him questioningly and he continued, "I know you and Jeb were having trouble, but it must be hard to hear people suspect him of murder."

"Not for me," Molly said. "I'm just surprised he's managed to live this long without anyone killing him."

"It's not the best thing, no," Ioana said. "I was wondering, Vampire Umpire, if you would mind taking me to dinner?" She ran her fingers slowly down his shoulder, and Molly felt jealousy gripe within her.

Molly entwined her fingers with Vampire Umpire's. "You can come to dinner with us if you want," she said. "We have a reservation for two at La Piastra di Grasso."

"The Italian place?"

"Yeah," said Molly. "It's not the best Italian restaurant in town, but it has the biggest portions." Her eyes lit up at the thought.

"That's okay," said Ioana, staring still at the couple holding hands before her. "I guess I will just see you at the tour brunch tomorrow?"

"You know it!" Molly said.

As they walked toward the restaurant, she said, "What was it you wanted to tell me before the press conference, Vampire Umpire?"

"Oh," he said. "Listen this is going to be hard to hear, and I am really sorry in advance okay? And I hope we can still be friends after, but know that I only did this because it mattered so much to me."

"You're scaring me," Molly said. "Just tell me and get it over with." She realised he had let go of her hand, and her own felt both cold and empty without it.

"I'm afraid I threw out your new sneaker," Vampire Umpire said. "You'd just walked through too many messes, and the smell was unbearable."

"You bastard," she said. "I could have cleaned them!"

"You could have," he said. "But we both know you would not have."

She glared at him for a while, but then said, "You're buying me *two* desserts tonight."

"Ha," he said. "I had intended to get you three."

♦

Late the next morning, Vampire Umpire's repose was disrupted by a call on his phone – Tyrone Ennis. "Vampire Umpire," he said. "It's an emergency."

"What's wrong?" he asked. "Is Molly okay?"

"Ms. Durand? Yes, she's fine, not sick at all" Tyrone Ennis said. "Apparently she was still too full from last night to eat much of the buffet."

"What?" Vampire Umpire said.

"Sorry, I'm unclear from panic. Let me explain," Tyrone Ennis said, then took an audible slow breath. "This morning we had the pre-Wimbledon brunch for all players and court staff," he began. "Everyone who has eaten the food has gotten some kind of terrible food poisoning."

"No, I deduced that from context," Vampire Umpire said. "I meant what? as in, how on earth was there a buffet but Molly ate none of it?"

"She did eat about two million lire in gelato…" Ennis said, thoughtfully.

"I guess she was just lucky," Vampire Umpire said. "She made me buy her four desserts last night."

"Well thank goodness," Tyrone Ennis said. "She's going to have to play an exhibition match today. With Moslius fled, she's the Wimbledon champion by default."

"Then what's the problem?" Vampire Umpire asked.

"Vampire Umpire, everybody else got sick. Everybody. You're the only umpire on tour any more. I can get untrained people to be linespeople, but the umpire is a sacred position."

"Then you're saying…?"

"Yes, Vampire Umpire. I want you to umpire the Wimbledon final for me after all."

"Will it be," Vampire Umpire said, "no strings attached, like a really terrible puppet show?"

"No strings," Tyrone Ennis said.

"Then you have an umpire."

◆

After he dressed in his umpire outfit, Vampire Umpire called Molly to ask her if she would postpone the match until night. There was no answer. He waited and then called again, but again there was no response. For the next hour and more he kept trying to the same lack of effect. Finally he called Tyrone Ennis and then left the hotel room.

He walked carefully down the corridors of the hotel, avoiding the odd patches of sunlight and deciding it would be unwise to take the glass elevator on the side of the building up to the penthouse suite. There he knocked on Jeb Moslius and Ioana Dumitrescu's door.

It was answered, by Ioana. "Can I come in?" he asked.

"Of course," Ioana said. Unconsciously she smoothed her hair, and her hands fluttered over the décolletage of her dress. Once they were both sitting, on the immensely comfy sofa that could be expected given the cost of the suite, she purred, "What can I do for you?" She placed her hand high on his thigh.

"Well," said Vampire Umpire. "I was wondering if you would release Molly from wherever you are keeping her?"

"What?" said Ioana. She sat straight now on the couch and her voice grew much cooler. "What are you talking about?"

"Molly. I want her now please," Vampire Umpire said.

"I don't have your asshole girlfriend," she sneered.

"Yes, you do. I'm pretty sure she's in the bathroom." He stood up and began walking over. "No, just stay there," he said as Ioana rose to follow him. "I'm happy to do this myself."

He opened the door and there found Molly tied up in the tub. He released her.

"Took you long enough," she said.

"I'm sorry, I was finishing my book," he said.

"How was it?"

"Longer than I thought," he said. "But I'm there now."

When they went back into the living room, Ioana was still sitting. "How did you know?" she asked.

"Oh, lots of reasons," Vampire Umpire said. "I knew the umpire hadn't been killed by a vampire. The complete loss of blood was an effect achieved by just placing the body in running water – from a stab wound, the flow of, for example, a river, will completely evacuate all the blood from any corpse. But what kind of person tries to suggest a murder has been committed by a vampire? Only someone from a culture where the nosferatu are common."

He walked over to the sofa and sat down. "And then all the subsequent attacks – all were either on Molly or could have been directed at her, and all after she had shown some small affection to me. And you were there for all of them."

Ioana suddenly reached down into the sofa and her hand reappeared holding a long, thin-bladed knife. She darted at Molly, swinging the knife fast in a vicious stabbing motion. She seemed to rebound off the air as off a wall. Vampire Umpire's hand had closed on her arm like a manacle.

"The athame is a witch's knife," Vampire Umpire said. "And after the curse, and that very particular stab wound Molly received, I would have figured it all out sooner. But I'm an umpire, not a detective, so it didn't seem like my job."

"Fine," Ioana said. "But if you don't let me go, I'll never tell you the spell I used to poison the coaching staff." She sneered at Molly. "Who'd have thought there would be a buffet where you wouldn't stuff your face like onions going up the fundament of a Christmas goose?"

"My appetite is healthy and adorable!" Molly protested.

"I agree," said Vampire Umpire.

Molly continued, "And I don't think that sucker punch you hit me with would have knocked me out so thoroughly if not for your reeking garlic perfume."

"Screw you," Ioana said. "And my threat still stands. All of them, all… will sicken and die in three days, if you don't let me walk out of here right now."

"I'm sorry," Vampire Umpire said, "but I have a friend who specialises in that kind of thing. He's already lifted your curse. Apparently it was a lot easier than the last one."

Ioana slumped on the coach and began to cry softly. "What I don't understand," said Vampire Umpire, "is why you did the first murder? The other attacks, they were because you had fallen for me, which humility makes hard to say. But why that first one?"

"You're such a great man," Ioana said, and she was clearly sincere. "Was it so bad that I wanted you?"

"You were with someone," Molly said. "Even if I assume Moslius is no better at sexy times than he is at tennis."

"Will you answer me?" Vampire Umpire said. "I told Tyrone Ennis to call the police after I had rescued Molly. They'll be here soon."

"Fine," Ioana said. "My family were once great nobles. My father lost our fortune creating the world's first garlic perfume, true. But he created it for a dual purpose: first the delightful alluring scent of garlic."

"That's seriously misjudged," Molly said. "Just a horrible business plan."

"And second to combat the scourge that destroyed my people!" Ioana continued, regardless.

"Your people?" Vampire Umpire asked.

"Centuries ago, my family were barons of a castle just outside Bucharest. But the noble son of an aged father came back bearing a dark and terrible curse."

Vampire Umpire and Molly both looked at each other in shock.

"He returned home afflicted. Immortal and timeless, yes. Strong, and brave as one who can know no pain. Tireless and vital and ceaseless. But he had become a terrible thing." Ioana paused and swallowed, fury blazing in her brown eyes. "He had become... an umpire!"

"What?" said Vampire Umpire.

"Whuck?" said Molly.

"The story has passed down my family from one generation to the next. The son returned as a noble vampire, bearing with him a fellow vampire who had afflicted him with the curse of umpirism. This diseased predator was known only as Umpire Vampire. And in their cruel depredations and ceaseless appetite for the torment and malice that only the umpiring of tennis matches can satisfy, the umpire branch of our family destroyed our standing, leaving the humans among us to suffer and scrape. So for generations we have waged war on the evil umpire. The umpire I killed, he was my first, and I waited only for the hunt for the killer to end before I would claim my next trophy. I will not call him a victim! For no umpire is deserving of even a second of life. And yet," she smiled sadly. "I have fallen in love with an umpire. It is my great tragedy."

"That is the worst case of Chinese whispers I have ever heard," Molly said.

"Can you say that?" Vampire Umpire asked. "Isn't it racist?"

"I don't think so – the etymology only requires the language to be one not widely understood in the presiding cultural milieu," Molly said.

"I guess."

"The Americans call it Telephone," Molly said. "I could call it that if you like?"

"I suppose it would be a mild improvement," said Vampire Umpire. "But Telephone doesn't really capture the miscommunication element. A telephone transmits pretty clearly."

"It is problematic then," Molly said.

"Well the important thing is I knew what you meant," he said.

◆

They sat and waited with Ioana until Tyrone Ennis and the police came to take her away.

"I guess this means Moslius is innocent," Tyrone Ennis said.

"That ugly stupid bastard is about as innocent as Hitler," Molly said. "But it is true he didn't commit the murder."

It was at that moment that a walk in wardrobe door burst open and out toppled a man tied to a chair. Moslius was soon untied and ungagged.

"That's right I'm innocent," he said.

"What the hell are you talking about?" Molly asked.

"Yes, I am afraid I don't follow either," Tyrone Ennis said. While the transition might very well have been seamlessly accomplished in descriptive prose by an immensely skilled writer, untying the man had taken a few minutes and too much time had passed for Moslius' conversational gambit to be effective.

"Of the murder," he said.

"Yeah," said Molly. "But they'll still imprison you probably – infinity counts of BEING A JERK."

She expected Moslius to react, but he just smirked. "Let's settle this on the court, rather than in court," he said.

"You mean where I've easily beaten you every time?"

"Set it up, Ennis," Moslius rudely commanded Tyrone Ennis. "Oh, and Durand… I don't agree to any delays or pauses. No equally agreed on time outs, or breaks. So unless you want your boyfriend umpiring out in the noon-day sun, I guess you're going to have to forfeit." Moslius leaned in and whispered, "I heard a lot, in the closet."

"I bet you've spent most of your life in the closet," Molly said, but it was a reflex action. She was shocked. There was no way out. "Tyrone," she said. "I'm afraid I need to…"

"Request a new tennis racquet," Vampire Umpire said. "She damaged her other one in Indian Wells and it won't hold up, I fear."

"What are you doing?" she asked him. "You'll die."

"Trust me," he said. "Mr. Ennis, could you ensure these two get to the court? I will see you there in a few moments."

◆

Vampire Umpire stepped into the Chamber of Umpires and called over one of the replacement ball girls. "Hi," he said. "I'm Vampire Umpire. What's your name?"

"Roger," the boy said. He had chestnut hair a shade lighter than his eyes, and a strong chin. His air of intelligence was clear.

"Do you like tennis?"

"I do, y'know. Some day I want to be as great a tennis player as Molly Durand."

"That's a noble goal," said Vampire Umpire. "But totally unrealistic. No-one will ever be as good as her again."

"Okay," the boy said.

"But, y'know… Make an effort, I guess?"

"I sure will." The boy smiled up at Vampire Umpire. "Can I get you anything?"

"Yes," said Vampire Umpire. "I need you to bring me all the sunscreen in Wimbledon."

"Okay!" the boy said.

"No, wait," Vampire Umpire said. "Not all the sunscreen, just about 90%. Leave some for the rest of the staff." He paused and looked up thoughtfully. "They will also need some sun screen."

◆

Vampire Umpire climbed up the steps to his high chair and sat down. Thousands of people, filling the towering coliseum of Wimbledon's centre court began to applaud, wildly, and he gestured them to quiet. On the grass to his right, Molly stood holding her red and black racquet. She smiled at him discreetly, and bobbed the racquet in a small wave. To his left, Moslius stood slumped, as if defeat slowed him already.

"Play commencing on the championship game," Vampire Umpire said into the microphone on his chair. "Ms. Durand to serve."

He watched as her slender arm threw up the ball and her other coiled the racquet behind her head. He watched the smooth curve of her back as she whipped the racquet through the ball and served a perfect ace. And he wondered if he had ever been happier than in that moment.

Epilogue

The next morning, Molly woke early. She slipped out of Vampire Umpire's embrace as gently as she could, and perhaps would have managed not to wake him, if in her path to the bathroom she had not accidentally trodden on the Wimbledon Championship Trophy, slipped, and knocked over first the bedside lamp and then the table. "Morning," he said.

"Morning," she replied, and kissed him.

Quite a while later a knock at the door brought a delivery. There was a note to Molly, and a small parcel. The note read:

Molly,

I found this while I was sorting out the brunch incident. I think you might have some talent in this area, and I thought this might be something worth your study.

R

She unwrapped the parcel, which was a book, with the title The Picatrix Grimoire. She opened it, and it was a compendium of spells. She ran her fingers over the pages, and the ink felt so thick she could have traced the words in the dark.

"Interesting," she said.

"Well you'll have plenty of time to study it," said Vampire Umpire. "Wimbledon is only halfway through the year's tennis tour."

"True," she said.

"So…"

"So what?" Molly asked.

"So for now, you need to ensure you stay fit. And the best way to do that is to stay rested. So you should definitely come back to bed," Vampire Umpire said.

She leapt hard into his arms and their lips met with the ease of long and joyful practice.

THE END